Augusta A. Varty-Smith

Matthew Tindale

A Novel: Vol.III.

Augusta A. Varty-Smith

Matthew Tindale
A Novel: Vol.III.

ISBN/EAN: 9783337044206

Printed in Europe, USA, Canada, Australia, Japan

Cover: Foto ©Andreas Hilbeck / pixelio.de

More available books at **www.hansebooks.com**

MATTHEW TINDALE.

A Novel.

BY

AUGUSTA A. VARTY-SMITH,

AUTHOR OF "THE FAWCETTS AND GARODS."

IN THREE VOLUMES.
VOL. III.

LONDON:

RICHARD BENTLEY AND SON,

Publishers in Ordinary to Her Majesty the Queen.

1891.

(All rights reserved.)

CONTENTS OF VOL. III.

BOOK V. (*continued*).

CHAPTER   PAGE

III. Marah   1

IV. The Day of the Funeral   18

BOOK VI.

I. Good-bye, Sweetheart   39

II. The Laying Down of a Life   58

III. Flight   79

IV. Struggles   104

BOOK VII.

I. Links   131

II. The Last Night at the Garod Arms   150

III. I have sinned   178

iv   CONTENTS.

BOOK VIII.

CHAPTER   PAGE

   I. THE TRIAL 195

  II. THE TRIAL—*continued* 219

 III. WE REAP WHAT ANOTHER HAS SOWN 248

 IV. BONDAGE AND FREEDOM 266

BOOK IX.

  I. AFTER FIVE YEARS 278

MATTHEW TINDALE.

BOOK V.

(Continued.)

CHAPTER III.

MARAH.

WHEN Matthew left the inn, he walked with uncertain steps across the strip of pavement and worn grass that separated the Garod Arms from the road. This traversed, he continued on his way toward his home, stumbling some-times and catching his feet where there were no actual hindrances to his progress. When he came to the gable end of Joseph Hind's house, he raised his eyes, knowing when he had gone another twenty yards that he would be able, by turning his head, to see the outline of the window in Bella's sleeping-room, perhaps lighted up by her candle and with her shadow crossing and recrossing it. But he did not intend to look ; he did not wish to see anything at that moment which would bring her forcibly into his remembrance.

So he stumbled on through the starlight, dull, weary, and unable to grasp one distinct idea from the chaotic mass seething in his brain. To get home and throw himself upon his bed, where perhaps the blessed forgetfulness of sleep might come, was the one desire that possessed him.

At length reaching that part of the road where the smithy stands back from it a few paces, he lifted his eyes and saw, with a kind of outward sense, that his mother's lamp yet burned in the kitchen, and that in the window above, the light had not been put out in his sister's room.

As he looked a dazed kind of wondering came into his mind ; he was as a sleeper roughly awakened. Why were the two lights burning ? Was it not ten o'clock—late enough for every one to be in bed ?

Here the remembrance of the events of the past week rushed upon him—the life of horrid memories which had been crowded into the time boundaries of seven days—and he stumbled no longer, nor went in a waving course from side to side, but walked erect and steadily. He had been called from the confused hideousness of a dream into the sternness of its reality.

Maggie had been sick and ill since that Sunday afternoon when she returned from her fruitless errand to the quarry wood. Her limbs had ached, she told her mother; and there was a confused ringing of bells in her ears, and a rushing sound like the falling of water or the sighing and moaning of wind through the trees. She was hot all over, she said ; and yet she felt cold, and could not keep herself from trembling ; and her eyes and her forehead seemed to be pinned down into the pillow by a bar of lead. So the good mother spread extra blankets over her child, and bade her drink the warm gruel she brought her, and keep still and try to quieten herself to sleep. But as day after day passed, Mrs. Tindale wondered that Maggie seemed to get no nearer recovery; and that the assertion of each night, spoken very wearily, that in the morning she would get up, was seemingly never remembered till evening came, and then it was merely reiterated to be again forgotten, although there were no longer any complaints of aching limbs, nor of burning heats, nor of shiverings which shook the narrow bed. There was nothing the matter with her, she said; she was only worn out and wanting rest. Would they let her sleep? she asked; would they let her be alone? If she might sleep and be left to herself she knew she would get better, that is to say she would get better by degrees, so soon as she was able to throw off the effects of that cold miserable rain; it had soaked her through and through; it had chilled her to the bone. And so Mrs. Tindale wondering greatly to herself, had been but little in Maggie's room ; she tried to be contented by going with careful step up the stairs, and pausing with ear held to the key-hole, if it might be but to catch the faint echo of a sigh or the sound of moving bed-clothes. But at all times the room was perfectly silent, and Mrs. Tindale would come away uneasy and full of doubt.

All that the poor woman could do was to go carefully through the events of that Sunday night, when Maggie had been taken ill ; from the time when Bill Taylor had brought his strange piece of news, to the moment when, with basin and spoon in hand, her candle sputtering low down in its socket, she had stood repeating what she had just heard at her child's bedside. How Mr. Sidney Aschenburg had left his home and had not been seen since the previous day ; and that his hat had been found among some willow branches growing by the edge of the river ; and that Matthew had set off with the other men of the village to try to find the body of Mr. Sidney Aschenburg if he were drowned, as they began to fear. And then she pictured the sudden quietness that had fallen upon the figure which had hitherto turned restlessly on the bed; and how, after stooping down with the candle held that it might throw its fitful gleams upon the face half hidden by the bed-clothes, she had seen that her child had fainted.

It was very strange, Mrs. Tindale would think, for the girl could not have fainted because of the news that had been told her; for Maggie, as each succeeding day passed, failed to show any interest in what was causing such excitement in the village. She always seemed as if she never cared to hear anything about it; would only close her eyes and, putting her cheek upon the pillow, would tell her mother she wanted to go to sleep. Until at last Mrs. Tindale ceased to speak of Mr. Sidney Aschenburg.

But when all doubt concerning his fate was set aside, Mrs. Tindale had hurriedly opened the door of Maggie's room in her excitement, and burst in upon her with the news, and the girl had broken away from her stupor and, starting up, had stretched out her arms with a bitter cry, uttering only the words, "Mother, mother," and had then fallen back, white, open-eyed and motionless upon the bed. It was then that the poor woman had been filled with mingled feelings of astonishment and misgiving.

Mrs. Tindale had spoken of all these things to her son, and her eyes had been moist and her lips trembling. But she did not dare to tell him of the suspicion which had come vaguely to her mind. This prosaic son of hers would have called her foolish and non-sensical to suppose that a village girl could have given her heart to the young squire, who curvetted on his bay mare past her father's cottage, but who never so much as cast his eye upon their doorstep. This was the only thing upon which Mrs. Tindale had been reticent with her son; everything else concerning Maggie she had told him.

So when Matthew lifted up his eyes to the light in his sister's room, visions of her life, such as it had been during the past week, came floating before him.

Could she not get to sleep? he wondered, his eyes fixed with painful intensity upon the lighted window.

A sigh quivered between his lips, as he thought that an hour ago he would have said that no addition could be made to the burden which he carried. Then he laid his hand upon the latch and stepped in.

"I did not expect to find you up, mother," he said, as he knocked his feet against the step, more as an act of habit than of necessity, for there was no mud upon his boots. "Is Maggie worse that both lights are burning?"

"She's a deal livelier to-night. That's why I'se sittin' up. She wants to see ye afore ye go to bed."

"To see me!" and a pitiful, pleading expression came into Matthew's eyes. He had known that his first meeting with his sister—for they had not seen nor spoken to each other since the previous Sunday—would be to him the bitterest draught which he would have to drink, and he shrank instinctively, as, wearied out, he felt it being raised to his lips.

"Yes. It's mebbe nothin' partic'lar." Here Mrs. Tindale got up, pushing her chair against the wall, and then paused in the centre of the kitchen. She was wondering how much she could say, without betraying the foolish notion about Maggie and young Mr. Aschenburg which had got into her head.

"Are ye goin' to bed, mother?"

"Yes." Still Mrs. Tindale was doubtful what she could say without betraying herself. At last she remarked, in what was meant to be an indifferent tone, " I wadn't, if I were you, say anything about young Mr. Aschenburg—it might keep her from sleepin', ye know."

"Nay, mother. I shan't, if she doesn't." And Matthew felt as if a deep wound in his bosom had been torn by lacerating hands.

"Well, I just thought I wad tell ye. Good night, my lad."

"Good night." The son watched the figure of his mother, until it disappeared through the narrow doorway that opened at the foot of the stairs. Then for some minutes he sat with his face buried in his hands, until at last he got up wearily, and quietly prepared to follow her.

A lamp was burning on the dressing-table in his sister's room, the little speckled looking-glass throwing up a square patch of reflected light upon the ceiling. There was one rush-bottomed chair drawn up at the side of the bed, and on it were standing a piece of bread and a cup of milk. These were the things which Matthew saw as he pushed open the door and went into the room, for he kept his head turned away so that his eyes might not rest upon the low wooden bed, and upon the figure of his sister.

"Come nearer, Mattha. I had somehow forgotten about ye—an' that was very queer like, for I have always turned to ye in all my troubles. Come nearer, for I can't do with ye standin' so far away." Maggie spoke in a dull, lifeless tone, but steadily and quietly.

Then he turned and gazed at her, with a strained look of agony on his face.

"Sit down there, Mattha. See, there's room for ye on the edge of the bed."

He obeyed mechanically. So soon as he was seated, his strong frame became relaxed ; the shoulders drooped, and one hand was flung out upon the bed as if for support.

"Maggie, I'm done for," he began brokenly, and the sound of sobbing, the sobbing of a man in dire distress, broke through the room.

There was a movement of the bed-clothes, and the girl raised herself into a sitting posture, stretching out one weak hand toward the powerful one that lay upon the coverlet. But she could not reach it ; could only strive after it as if she would give it some gentle caressive touches.

"Oh, Mattha, Mattha," and her voice began

to tremble a little, though it was still lifeless and cold. "Dear old chap—what is the matter? I'm getting better. Ye needn't be a bit afraid about me." Then, because a sharp sting of remorse struck her for not having asked to see this brother, and such a brother as he had ever been to her, throughout the week, she began to cry a little in a helpless, childish kind of way.

But Matthew made no reply; only bowed himself, with his face hidden from her, at the foot of the bed.

"Mattha, what is it?" And there was something of an impatient wail in the tone in which the question was put.

There was an attempt to hide the signs of unusual emotion; a lifting up of the bowed head; a checking of the sobbing until it became inaudible, and a straightening of the shoulders that had heaved so convulsively. And then Matthew said tremblingly, and with lips that were parched and clung together, "I meant to care for ye, God knows. And here have I done worse for ye than any man."

The girl remained motionless, her eyes fixed upon the figure of her brother as he sat where it was sharply outlined by the light of the lamp. The tears ceased running down her cheeks, the expression of weakness on her face slowly gave way to one of troubled wondering surprise, which deepened until her pale lips parted, and her large dark eyes opened widely with a look of fear, that gradually and almost imperceptibly passed into one of horror. She clutched the bed-clothes tightly with both hands, her breath coming with a laboured sound, as though she were trying to speak but failed. Then at length in a whisper, in which her lips seemed to be battling against her will and refusing to give utterance to any sound, she said, " Did you—did you and him—Mr. Sidney Aschenburg—you said you quarrelled." And then her voice failed.

There was no reply, save a shrinking back of the man's strong frame, and a putting up of one hand as though he were warding off a blow.

A long pause followed; and then the girl leaned toward her brother. For several seconds she essayed to speak; but not so much as a whisper broke the silence of the room. At length, with eyes dilated and shining, words came dropping between each catching of her breath, which were perfectly distinct and audible.

The man slowly raised his eyes and looked at her. She could not see the waxen hue of his face, nor the hollow between the eyebrows and upon each cheek. Only the familiar outline of his head against the wall, and the straight and well-shaped neck and shoulders. But he could see the ravages which a week's sorrow had worked upon her face, upon the once rounded cheeks and delicately formed lips.

Again the words came from her, and were spoken less hesitatingly and in a firmer tone, for she had caught at the straw of hope which his silence gave.

" Mattha—was 't you 'at pushed him in ?"

The man swayed and would have fallen toward her, had he not again thrown out the arm by which he propped himself upon the bed. His breath came in laboured gasps, his utterance was inarticulate as he said, " Maggie, God knows I have repented." His voice failed, and he leaned forward helplessly, looking at her.

For a moment she did not move, her eyes fixed, her lips parted, her thin face pallid with the agony of this new horror. Then she suddenly flung her hands and arms out of her brother's reach, and shrank back into the farthest corner of the bed, an expression of loathing and detestation coming into her face.

" Go away, Mattha—go away. I feel a'most as if I hate ye."

Matthew had risen from the bed, and now stood drawn up to his full height; but there was none of the old pride in his bearing,

only the look of one who has resolutely braced
himself up to endure.

"I willn't ask ye to forgive me, Maggie"
—the speaker's voice was low and husky—
"I can never expect that. But will ye
not say one word to me—just one word,
Maggie, to take away a little of my
misery?"

But she made no answer; only held to the
same shrinking attitude and expression of
loathing and horror.

"Must I go, Maggie?" There was a
plaintive complaining ring in the words; and
the speaker swept his great muscular hand
with an abandoned gesture across his eyes and
forehead.

He waited for fully half a minute, but she
made no answer. Then a spasm of agony
came into his face, and he turned away with
a sudden movement. Could he complain, if
she, the sister whom he had loved and ever
tenderly guarded, abandoned him in this the
hour of his sin and shame? And with this

thought settling like the chill of death upon his heart he sought the door, and without a word or so much as one glance backward, went out of the room.

CHAPTER IV.

THE DAY OF THE FUNERAL.

THEY laid him in his last resting place—the handsome young master of Derthwaite—with the pale October sunshine spreading across the churchyard and throwing tiny shadows from the graves. An old friend of the family buried him, who on first hearing the news of the Derthwaite calamity had written, begging to be allowed to come if he could be of any service. This offer had been accepted with a curious unbending by Mrs. Aschenburg, who wrote herself to say that if such an old and valued friend would read the funeral service over her boy, she would be grateful.

The sun shone upon the graves, and upon the red sandstone church, lichened and weather-beaten; but there was no warmth in its rays, for the wind had got into the east and blew clear and keen. Men and women stood in groups, wherever a door or wall afforded shelter from observation, to watch the long black procession as it moved out of the lane and came into the village street; those who had at first smoked and talked and bandied vulgar jests, coming gradually under the influence of that quietness and solemnity which death brings with it.

The man whom every one knew would be the new master of Derthwaite was there; for years ago had it not always been said by Dr. Joseph Aschenburg, that after his son, the cousin whom he had chosen to be his son's guardian, would be the heir to the property and estates. He was leaning back in the first carriage, so that as the procession passed, not a man or woman caught a glimpse of his face. But this mattered little, for they

could picture quite easily the straight upright
figure; the glossy white hair; the clean-shaven
face; the blue-grey eyes; the placid expression
with its suggestiveness of strength, though
doubtless this might be somewhat disturbed
by the trouble and sorrow, which every servant
about the place had not been slow to assert,
had been brought to Mr. Aschenburg by the
death of his young cousin and sometime ward.

And then came a long row of carriages;
after them the Derthwaite work-people and
servants. Old Willie was there—the gardener
who had tried to teach Sidney, when quite
a baby, to love flowers—holding to the arm
of his big stalwart son who was now gardener
in his stead, audibly grumbling the while
at the "rheumatics" that made walking so
difficult a feat; and then at death that was
"so unlevel in its wayses," as to take off his
young master and leave *him* with his grey
hairs and aches and pains.

Walker and Dodd, the gamekeepers, had
to shorten the strides to which their long

legs were accustomed, so that no discomfort might come to old Willie's heels. Their minds being at ease with regard to their future prospects, they were in a good enough humour to bear this temporary inconvenience; for so long as pheasants and hares had to be preserved on the Derthwaite estate, they had argued together upon the day when the clear beautiful river had parted its waters to give up a strange and unseemly burden, so long would gamekeepers be wanted; and if game-keepers, why not Walker and Dodd. And so now at the funeral, they had nothing to talk about which could rival in interest the new method by which partridge eggs could be more satisfactorily hatched.

Behind these two came Tom and "Nailer," the stable boys, the name of the latter being due to the pithy and epigrammatic way he had of closing a sentence. They had both walked for the most part, silently in the procession; Tom chiefly occupying himself by taking thoughtful surveys of the horizon, when he had to blink his eyes very often in order to clear away the mistiness by which the landscape was dimmed to him. "He was a grand un"—the Nailer had said once or twice—"and if he was a bit haffly in his ways, what of that—better have a crooked branch than a crooked root; folks could see the one and mind their heads, but the other would trip them up by their feet." And each time the Nailer spoke his collar became suddenly tight, and one of the hands which had only with the utmost difficulty been pushed into the undertaker's black gloves, was put up to relieve the pressure. At this point Tom's eyes always opened and closed very rapidly, and a sweeping glance had to be taken from the Pennine range to the mighty Helvellyn.

The two men immediately behind talked of the rotation of crops, and wondered, now that Mr. Sidney was gone, whether Mr. Aschenburg would be willing to let them plough the little bit of lea behind the kitchen gardens—Mr.

Sidney would ; he was an easy one to manage.
And here the conversation changed, because of
the halt made at the church gates.

The ceremony was soon over.   The polished
oak case, together with the white wreaths that
covered it were lowered into the grave, a
handful of soil being thrown on to the flowers,
which crushed them and the tender maiden-
hair ferns.   Then came the pressure, slight
and respectful among the Derthwaite retainers,
to get near that open space, each set of men
taking turn and turn about, to pass round
the grave.   Old Willie's lameness was very
perceptible, in spite of the help of the strong
son's arm, as he stumbled over the loose earth ;
and big tears ran down his withered cheeks,
while he said something querulously, and
which was only half intelligible, about his
young master and the " rheumatis." And
then his son forcibly pulled him away, and
took him carefully between the green mounds
toward the churchyard gates.   Walker and
Dodd, together with half a dozen farm

labourers, looked silently down at the flowers —but they never saw beyond the flowers; they thought only of the pure white petals and the maiden-hair, not of the heart which had so lately beaten with all the restless energy and passion of youth. Behind them stood Tom with his hands in his pockets, and his back turned upon the men who were moving slowly round the grave. His mind was occupied with the way in which "the young master" had gently administered reproofs to him during his three years of service, pointing out the curb chains, which had not been quite so bright as Tom's sinewy hands might have made them, the saddles that had been loosely girthed, the tardiness with which Tom had been wont to respond to the young master's call—how Tom wished he had gone the very instant he had heard the familiar voice—these things, and a score of other stable misdemeanours, which had always been pointed out without a frown or an oath. And Tom's eyes smarted, and strove

yet more assiduously to distinguish the outline
of the most distant hills. How he wished
he had been a better lad ! and how he wished
he could see his young master, if but for
one moment, to tell him this, and ask his
forgiveness! And then the Nailer came from
the grave-side to him, and gave him a push
in his side, which, though done with roughness,
was meant to be kind. " Come, I say," said the
Nailer, in a low husky voice, while he struggled
with his collar, " come, an' look in. Ye'll be
sorry if ye don't, for it's last t' look you'll
ever get of him. Come—I can see his face as
fair as if there was no coffin-lid." And the
two turned and went toward the line of soil,
and the shadow-filled cleft beyond. "Good-
bye, master," said the Nailer, in a choking
tone, so soon as he and his fellow stable-boy
were bending down and looking into the
grave—" Good-bye." And then, because Tom's
eyes could no longer see the sky-line, the
tears welled over his lids, and fell like splashes
of rain upon the coffin and upon the flowers.

"Amen," he said, making a violent effort to overcome his emotion, so that he could speak, and thus not have his devotion outdone by the Nailer; "Amen, master; I would give all my wages to have been a better lad." And then they pushed their hands into their pockets, and turning hurriedly away, stumbled as poor old Willie might have done, their thoughts too much occupied with imaginings of the quiet face they knew to be beneath the coffin-lid, to care now about hiding their emotion. What did it matter to them if their fellow-servants saw them weeping—had they not lost their master, and were not their thoughts all turned upon him? And those who had talked of the rotation of crops, picked up a handful of the loose earth near the grave, examining it attentively, and remarking that it would "be grand for either swedes or mangolds." Then they threw it down carelessly; and because the old sexton had begun his gruesome task, they turned the broadsides of their boots and helped to push in the soil, heedless of the flowers and of what lay beneath. Barley and wheat were alone full of interest to them—a living dog was of more account to them than a dead lion.

In a little time the blinds were drawn up and the curtains pulled back from the windows at Derthwaite, and the chill cold-looking sunlight was let in.

An air of vacancy hung over all the rooms, a broadly written truism upon each blazing hearthstone and cushioned divan, that something had gone from them that would never return. The silence that had been like a pall over the house for four sombre days, could not readily be broken; a door closing hastily caused a jarring sound, and those who spoke felt it must still be done in whispers. A feeling of inertness hung over every one; the slow steady course of ordinary life had been suddenly arrested, and it seemed as though it must be a little while before the torpor

could pass away, and the flow of daily life set
in again.

The servants were the first to rise against
this feeling. The cook had an extra pint of
beer drawn for herself, and when she had
swallowed it at a draught, diligently endeavoured to raise her spirits, or, as she termed
it, " to shake herself; " after which she promised
that there should be savoury dishes that night
for supper, and if any one " had a mind " to
choose for himself or herself what they should
be, she would be glad to listen to them.
Sparkes the butler tried to dissipate the
gloom by a brandy and soda; and began to
lecture his subordinates upon the desirability
of keeping a cheerful countenance at all times.
In the still-room a good deal of tea was
drunk—the dairy-maid having been first
despatched to bring some of the thickest of
cream. Even Juno, the Gordon setter, lifted
up her intelligent head, her nostrils moving
eagerly and her tail wagging, when she saw
the blinds being drawn up in the housekeeper's

room; and as she followed close upon the heels of the footman who drew up the blinds in one room after another, she began to think it was a new sort of game invented expressly for herself—for Juno was not so many months removed from puppyhood—and gamboled in a half circle behind the man, taking care however to keep as much to heel as such careering would allow.

" Down dog, will you "—was said once or twice in a low tone, but fault-finding went no further than that; for Juno had belonged to the young master who had but just been carried from the house, and an unusual feeling of sentiment had taken possession of the man.

From the drawing-room to the breakfast-room they went, and then to the library and long dark dining-room ; and here Juno gave yelps of delight, and bounded up to try to catch this good play-fellow's hand as the curtain-rings rattled and the shutters were folded and put back. " You stupid ! Don't you know you've lost your best friend ? " expostu-

lated the footman, his face and voice full of
sadness as the form of his young master rose
before him.   But Juno only bounded the
more and gave sharper yelps of delight.   And
then they came to the last room in which
the man was to let in the cold meaningless
sunlight; and he paused on the threshold
before he could make up his mind to enter
that place, which had in an especial sense
been given up to his master's use.   Here Juno
forgot about her merry gambols. This was
the room in which she was accustomed to
find her soul's beloved; and ah! how had
it been that she had been separated from him
for so many days?   "Turn the handle
quickly," her eyes pleaded; and she put her
nose to the ground and began to scratch
and to whine; *he* at least would let her in;
he would never be deaf to her cry.

The man turned the handle, and the dog
bounded past him into the closely curtained
room.

The crimson hangings which fell from the

middle of the ceiling across the apartment had for some reason or other been drawn closely, thus cutting off one-half of the room from the other. To Juno, however, they offered but a slight impediment, and, with a curious mixture of leapings and wrigglings, she contrived to push her way past them. "You'll be upsetting something, I suppose," exclaimed the footman to himself, as, without waiting to let the light into the first half of the apartment, he stepped hurriedly after the dog, vexed with himself for having admitted it where chairs and tables were always littered with all kinds of odds and ends, and where it was easy in a moment for a dog to work dire destruction. Quickly and more easily than Juno he found the divisional line of the curtains, and, lifting one slightly, bent his head to pass beneath it, when astonishment at what he saw arrested his movements.

The curtain of the farthest window had been pushed aside, and the sunlight was shining upon the carpet, and across the

writing-table at which Sidney would often
sit, and upon the morocco-covered arm-chair
which was his, and which had now been
turned with its side to the table.

In this chair was a slight girlish figure.

" Oh, Juno, Juno, we both loved him ! "

The passionate exclamation was broken
with tears, and rendered indistinct by the
speaker hiding her face against the dog which
had bounded up to her.

The man instantly dropped the curtain.
Here was something which he was not meant
to see—a grief in which he could have no
part; and quietly, but with hasty steps, he
made his way out of the room, a tightened
feeling about his heart.

Upstairs, in the room that was decorated
with peacocks and roses and vines, on the
deep, old-fashioned couch which had been
drawn in front of the fire, sat Sidney Aschenburg's mother, through his death no longer
mistress of Derthwaite. Her silk skirts
heavily trimmed with crape were spread out

in an amplitude of folds; but not so far, however, as to prevent Abel, who was also seated on the couch, from giving caressing touches from time to time to the broad, handsome shoulders, and from holding one of the cold white hands within her own.

The two had been talking together for an hour past. All the oft-told nursery stories relating to Sidney had been gone through again; any action belonging to his boyish days which told of kindness had been dwelt upon. The gaiety, the light-heartedness, the good humour, even the careless vivacity had been praised; and then the mistress had broken into a paroxysm of weeping. She had not loved him enough, she told Abel, her head resting on the old nurse's shoulder: her memory was full of thorns. It seemed that she had only and ever been reserved and distant and proud, had never let it be known that deep down in her heart there was a germ of devotedness to him. "But oh, Abel," she said, "it was a proud kind of devotedness!

I wanted him to excel in all things. I wanted to see him admired and courted for his talents, and for some real work which he had done in the world. And instead of that, he was a failure."

But the old nurse kissed the tear-stained cheek and would not hear the word.

Meanwhile, on the moor above Staneby, upon one of the unenclosed patches of ground where the heather still grew, and where lay big boulders lichened and time-worn, a man paced with uneven steps. His face had grown thinner since the night he had ordered "glasses round" at the Garod Arms, raising an empty one to his own lips and drinking from it as though unaware that its foaming contents had been drained long ago. He had come up from the village because he could not bear the sight of that long black procession which would pass his doorway. He had closed the shutters of the smithy, and had said that he would do no stroke of work for that morning at least; and his mother and

father had acquiesced, thinking he but paid
a proper tribute of respect to the young
master of Derthwaite. After that he set off
to the moor, feeling as if he wanted space in
which to breathe, and miles of country round
him over which he could stride unchecked.
And up there for a time he seemed to be
alone, only the occasional twittering of a
yellow-hammer, the scuttering of a rabbit,
and the soft steady swish of the heather and
the few dwarfed trees as the east wind blew
on them, breaking upon the stillness of the
scene. But afterwards there came a sound
clear and distinct, then softened, and then
again so faint as scarcely to be heard, and
then wholly carried away by the breeze. The
man started, pausing for a moment like an
animal pursued ; and then, with a fierce kind
of energy, tramped through heather and
gorse, crushing down their growth heedless
alike of twigs and thorns. But still the sound
followed him, until the tolling of the bell
which was ringing at his victim's funeral

seemed to fill the air. On he went. Presently he retraced his steps. But still the sound pursued him, only louder, until the far distant tolling rang like clarion-notes upon his ear.

An hour had passed since first he heard the tolling of the bell; and then he knew that the same sense which played him false, and at times filled the air with sounds as of men breathing hard in some contest of life and death, of the scraping of feet upon the edge of a rock, and then the cry of one appealing to his God, was the same sense which even now was playing with delusive mockery upon his ears. A shudder passed through his frame. Was another sound to be added to those phantom ones by which he was haunted? No answer came, and his face grew grey in the cold light of the afternoon.

For several minutes he stood irresolute, and then turned his face toward Staneby. What could it matter? The bell would ring on, whether he was on the moor or in the smithy;

but if he were in the smithy, he could add a
material clashing to its din, and it might be,
that the one would cause the other to die
down.   And so he passed through the heather,
and beyond the stunted thorn-bushes, until
he came upon the road which led from the
scattered farm-houses on the fell-side, to the
village.

But what was that which followed closely
in his track, moving warily where there was
nothing but the low growth of heather, and
then making a momentary pause behind some
boulder, in order that the secure shelter of a
broken bit of ground could with more certainty
be reached?   A pursuing thing which rubbed
its grimy hands in satisfaction, and chuckled
aloud to itself, thinking that it alone perhaps,
in the whole universe, possessed the secret by
which the man's pacing to and fro on the
moorland, and his evident agitation of mind
could be explained.   The thing laughed aloud,
and thrust its hands under the folds of black
calico twisted round its waist, as it thought to

itself, that if it were but able to track the man down, shoemaking and poaching might be given up, perhaps, for the rest of its days.

As the man went toward Staneby, a girl rose from her bed, with wan cheeks and sunken eyes.   A trouble had to be planned for and met, and it was no use lying there.

When the finality of hope comes, there is always something if one will only look for it, which will effectually put a stop to the selfishness of despair.

BOOK VI.

CHAPTER I.

GOOD-BYE, SWEETHEART.

" WHILE the earth remaineth, seed-time and harvest, and cold and heat, and summer and winter, and day and night shall not cease."

Matthew stretched his arms above his head wearily.

He was standing in the doorway of the smithy, watching with eyes that were dull and listless, the angry-looking bank of clouds in the west. There were no flecks of crimson, no rosy bars lying upon opal, no threads of golden light; all was dark, lurid and massive —a typical November sunset.

He had been at work all day; standing
at the anvil several hours before the sun
had shown itself in the east. But although
he had laboured continuously, trying to give
his whole attention and strength to the thing
which he had in hand, he was but working
with the apathy of the hireling. He took
no pleasure in his task; the clever artificer
had lost his cunning, the felicitous touch was
gone, the iron would no longer take the old
beautiful curves.

Was it to be always thus, he wondered,
with the slow painfulness of one whose mental
powers are numbed, while his eyes mechanically followed the outline of a cloud? Was he
never again to love his work? Was nothing
ever again to be a joy to him? Were the
days only to be filled with weariness, rounded
off by what always seemed but a momentary
forgetfulness? Was this to go on continually
from sunrise to sunset?

It was then that he had stretched his arms
above his head in an action expressive of

physical and mental weariness, and the solemn and prophetic words had beaten like the dull notes of a dirge upon his mind. The assurance of perpetuity concerning the vast gyrating universe, fastened itself upon the round of his own life, and sealed the continuity of its suffering. Was there always to be this dragging out of days? Were the summers and winters, and cold and heat, and seed-time and harvest to have no end?

There must have been something in the slowly creeping twilight, in the unwonted cessation of work, and because he was standing with empty hands in the doorway, that caused Matthew's thoughts to become gradually associated with Bella Hind. How often had he stood in the doorway at sundown, waiting impatiently for her to come past. First, he would catch the sound of her voice as it called " How, how ; " and then Daisy would come, or perhaps Blackie or Roany round the turn in the lane, and lastly, Bella herself, daintily tripping. He had not spoken to

Bella since that day when they had walked home together from the moor. But he had seen her go past the smithy from the place where he stood at the anvil, and had watched her hungrily, knowing that even if she looked at him, the darkness of the forge would hide the expression of his eyes from hers. He had never gone to the window or the door when he had seen her glance toward the smithy from under her sun-bonnet, although he fancied her step became slower, and that she even loitered in her walk; twice, indeed she had stooped down, and was fully a minute in making the clasp of her clog secure.

But how could he speak now to Bella? The dream which had come to him through the summer months, tremblingly at first, until it had glowed and palpitated before him with the colours of life, had been suddenly and violently dispersed. The love in his heart remained; but the dream was gone. The memory of Bella used to fill the morning air with a sweetness greater than belonged to it alone; and the sun shone more brightly and the flowers had more gorgeous colouring ; even the tasks which he took in hand went more easily and merrily because of her. But this was all changed. The dream of making Bella his wife had vanished ; from henceforth there must be no thought of marriage for him ; he must set himself apart, because of the events of that one night which had put upon him the mark of Cain.

And so he stood in the doorway of the smithy, his eyes mechanically travelling along their accustomed path where Bella's cows used to come round the turning in the lane ; he knew that they would not come now, for the evenings were chilly and Joseph Hind was careful of his cattle. And yet he stood waiting for them like a man in a dream.

Faintly, and with intervals of several seconds when no sound could be heard because of the feet of the walker treading upon grass, came the sound of footsteps from the opposite direction from that in which Matthew was abstractedly gazing. He did not hear it, so deeply was he wrapped in thought. When, however, the feet trod where the grass was worn bare by horses and men on their way to the smithy, and rang upon the hard road, Matthew started, turning round with the expression of dread which of late mere trifles called up into his face. He always started now at any unexpected sound ; if any-one spoke to him suddenly, he would turn upon them with a nervously strained attention; if a bar of iron slipped unexpectedly from the anvil, or if the breeze catching up a handful of dead leaves whirled them against the wooden shutters of the smithy window, his grip would be closer upon the tool that he had in his hand, and he would give that visible and sudden movement of the body which tells of nerves tightly strung.

When he saw that it was Bella who had stepped off the road and was coming toward him, he would have turned into the smithy and so have avoided her, but for that careful-

ess which was growing with him concerning
ach look and act.

Bella had been disturbed and troubled about
Matthew's never coming to see her father on
hat Sunday evening when he had promised;
intil hearing the news which had been brought
iy the water-watcher to the village, she was
atisfied, and easily explained Matthew's
bsence to herself. Of course he would be
ine of the very first to be told the news—he
vas always called upon in time of emergency—
ind certainly he would not shrink from what
vas so evidently a duty, even when a visit to
ier weighed in the other side of the balance.
So she argued with herself, and was well-
pleased to think that Matthew must have set
off to join one of the search parties that had
peen formed, for of course he must have done
his, or else he would have come to them and
iave been found comfortably smoking with
ier father when the news had been brought to
he Hinds. Besides, he could not have meant
to trifle with her, for had he not smiled kindly

and pleasantly at her when he made the promise? But as the days went by and she saw nothing of Matthew, not even when she passed the smithy, she became a little anxious again, and went through the events of that Sunday evening, until a doubt worked itself into her mind, and she wondered whether, after all, there might not have been plenty of time for Matthew to have stepped across the green to their house, before hearing the news that had roused the village. Bella could not tell how the truth lay; and she thought over the puzzle until her head ached and her heart became sore and restless. At last she determined that she would make an errand which would take her past the forge, taking care that it should be at a time when possibly Matthew might have slackened work a little, and, perhaps, even be standing for a moment's rest within the doorway.

Therefore, when Bella, coming through the growing shadows, saw Matthew standing as she had pictured him, her heart gave a leap of gladness; and, after a momentary pause of hesitation, while she wondered whether he could deem her wanting in maidenly modesty if she stepped off the road to greet him, she began to pick her way over the uneven ground which led to the smithy door.

" It's late, Bella, surely for ye."

Although Matthew had been thinking of her, and had seen her little tripping figure coming toward him twenty times down the lane, yet when he turned round and actually saw her he was startled.

" Ay, it's late," returned Bella hesitatingly; "but t' days is short ye see, an' where there's only one woman in a house there's a deal to be done. I was just going up to Derthwaite Lodge, but when I saw ye I thought I wad step down an' ask after Maggie."

The last sentence had really been planned by Bella long before she left home as an excuse for stopping to speak to Matthew, should she be fortunate enough to see him, only she had always said it over to herself with a smile and shy drooping of the head, for somehow she could always imagine she was in Matthew's presence, and talking to him. Now, however, there had been something in the tone of his voice which had struck a chill to her, and she held up her head and looked with a startled expression into his face.

"She's going about again. I think she's all right."

Matthew's sorrowful gaze went to the red cloud which was paling into a sombre mass, not seeing it however, for his mind had gone to the sister to whom he had never spoken since that night when she had shrunk away into the farthest corner of her bed, and had waved him from her; never spoken to her— that is, but to make the few ordinary remarks which would shield their estrangement from observation. And Maggie had never spoken to him, saving in the same way and for the like reason. And each had taken care that their eyes should never meet.

The coldness and want of sympathy in

Matthew's manner filled Bella with uneasiness, She would have liked there and then to have turned and left him, for he pained her. Yet to have done that, Bella, with her woman's tact, knew would be dangerous, feeling instinctively that the coldness was not feigned as she sometimes feigned coldness from a kittenish desire to tease her lover, but was real and directed actively against herself, so that to leave him at that particular juncture would be the opening up of a quarrel that perhaps might never be healed.

"I'm glad Maggie's better," Bella remarked, feeling that something, no matter of how trivial a nature, must be said to break the pause which had followed Matthew's reply to her question. "I havin't heard of her since last Saturday, for Mrs. Tindale rarely gets down the village. And as for ye, a body might think ye were in hidin' for the few times one sets eyes on ye nowadays."

The last words were spoken with an attempt at jocularity, nevertheless they caused Matthew to start violently and give a suspicious look at Bella. Then he answered briefly, saying that he had been busier than usual, and had kept closely to the smithy.

"Ay, ye seem to get busier instead o' hevin' less to do."

"Work's about iverything." And as Matthew said this he turned his eyes with a weary expression from Bella, and looked far away over the valley.

What should she do, she wondered; should she talk to him of indifferent things and then leave him with a cheerful good night, as though no shadow had come between them? or should she ask what was amiss with him, and tax him with unkindness? But Bella's little heart was growing heavy, and to simulate cheerfulness would be difficult; while, on the other hand, it seemed almost impossible for her to speak openly of the change in his manner, pride lest he should see she loved him preventing her in the first instance; and secondly, the fear of breaking down her barrier of maidenly reserve by some ill-chosen word or faltering tone. It would be easier to go back to the experience of a few weeks ago, and speak of that unfulfilled promise of the Sunday evening's visit. Besides, all that had troubled her seemed as if it could be dated from that evening. And so Bella, after a little hesitation, began—

"Mattha, mebbe ye'll think shame o' me for being so plain spoken, but there's a thing that I've got on my mind which I'd like to ask ye about." She thought she saw a change in the expression of his face as though her words were disagreeable to him, but she could not be sure, for the twilight was deepening, and the dull red light which had been shining out of the west was gone, so she continued steadily, "I've never see ye since that day you an' me met on t' moor, an' ye asked me something about coming to hev a pipe with father t' next evening. D' ye mind ?"

"I mind every word you said to me, Bella."

" Well, you never came."

Matthew remained silent, his face immovable—she could see that, in spite of the
growing darkness.

" Ye never came," she repeated, no effort
being made on his part to reply. " An' I wad
ha' thought nothing about it "—here Bella
unconsciously wandered from the truth—" if
I'd seen ye two or three times between that
day an' this, an' if ye'd been just the same as
ever."

There was a momentary pause; and then
Matthew said, quietly and unhesitatingly, that
he had changed his mind about coming, and
had thought it better to stay away. During
the pause Matthew's eyebrows were slightly
drawn together as if he were suffering, and
then the forehead had smoothed itself as he
spoke to Bella. He was standing with his
hands spread out and resting on his hips, his
shoulders thrown back, his head up, and as
though he rather held himself away from the
girl than toward her while he talked. His

bearing, the very attitude in which he stood, had undergone an indescribable change since that day they had walked home together from the moor. And this change Bella was not slow to mark. So far she had only believed they were on the verge of a lover's quarrel, but at this instant the chill struck her which comes when a woman first stands face to face with the knowledge that the power hitherto wielded by her over some man is shaken, and that there is danger of it passing altogether from her hands. Instantly, she comprehended her position, and because hope was struck from her, she began to fence weakly.

"It was not kind of ye, Mattha. I got supper ready, an' I told father that he might expect ye, an' it made a kind o' fool o' me."

"It isn't often I go away from our own fireside, unless it is to the Garod Arms for a little bit."

"But we're old neighbours."

"I'm too busy to mind about my neighbours."

The listless tone in which these words were said went with a pang to Bella's heart. It seemed to her that he was in trouble about something. And oh, what would she not give to comfort him! And then, because she knew of no way to help him than that which pours out its own trouble by way of sympathy, she broke out with the words—

"Oh, Mattha, ye're vexed with me about something. I see it as fair as fair. Ye're not pleased to see me one single bit this evening."

"I'm pleased to see ye, Bella, very pleased." There was a faint ring of tenderness in his voice, and he began to shift his weight uneasily from one foot to the other. "I've known ye ever since ye were a little 'un, an' I reckon I'll always be ready to look out an' give ye a nod in passin', same as I've always done."

"What do ye mean, Mattha?" Bell felt as if she were confronting some hideous enormity which she could not comprehend; and her voice failed her a little in speaking.

"I mean just what I say. I'm glad to see

ye ; very glad. An' it 'll always be the same with me."

Bella saw that her dream of the summer months was over, and from henceforth she would be no more to Matthew Tindale than a butterfly upon the breeze. Then she made one last desperate effort.

"Mattha, ye've been unkind to me—ye've played me false."

There was a long pause; and then the man broke it, speaking in husky tremulous tones. But his attitude was unchanged. He still stood upright and unbending.

"Bella," he said—and there was a caress in the very way he spoke the word—"I've been true to ye, and never truer to ye than I am at this moment. Go away, my little girl. Take care of yerself. Good night, and God bless ye."

But here Bella's little heart, that had been filled with tears for some time back, suddenly strengthened itself with pride and anger. It was just because Matthew had inherited old

Mark Tindale's money, and had grown proud and considered himself above her, that he had dared to jilt her in this way, and for a minute she could not speak. Then she said, in a voice that was intended to show how light a thing it was to her to have fallen from his favour—

"Well, I think I must not stand talkin' any longer or I'll never get to Derth'aite. Father always says I wad talk to a broomstick if it hed a hat on. You'll tell Maggie I asked after her? An' if ye'll tell her that any night she likes to come an' see my new patch-work quilt, she's welcome. I did say I wad bring it up to her; but I'm beginning to think it's too much of a lump to carry.

"I'll tell her what ye say, Bella."

"Well, good night." The girl turned slowly away from him as she said this, tears rising in her voice in spite of her brave words. "It's goin' to be a grand evening after all. Look at that star." And she raised her hand as she spoke.

It seemed to her that he was a little while in answering. Then he briefly returned her "good night," no notice being taken by him of the star to which her finger pointed. Bella could see that much, in spite of the growing darkness; he had not even turned his head to look at it. Then she stepped away from him, stifling the bitter angry sobs which shook her frame. He had jilted her, she kept repeating to herself as she walked along the Derthwaite road. He had been amusing himself with her through all the summer months, and had never meant anything with all his fine looks and words.

Poor little Bella! It would have puzzled her very much could she have known that the man she had left wrapped in a cloak of seeming indifference, stood hungry-eyed peering after her into the gloom, his ears strained to catch each sound of her footsteps, his hands wringing his leathern apron in distraught womanish fashion.

CHAPTER II.

THE LAYING DOWN OF A LIFE.

MATTHEW kept closely to his forge in those days at the beginning of November.

The lawyer at Merton sent him a letter saying that the advertisements had been withdrawn from the American papers, and strongly urged him to give up the search for Tom Tindale's widow and child. It was useless, so the letter said, to prosecute a search which was both hopeless and suicidal; and, because the store of sovereigns was spent, Matthew yielded. He ceased to have any interest in the finding of the rightful owner of the property; he no longer took a pride in the advertisements; he never seemed to

feel the old necessitous pressure of a walk
to Merton, in order that he might have a few
satisfying words with the lawyer; he had
given up thinking about it, or, if he did, it
was only in a dull, stupid kind of way.

He had begun to go oftener to the Garod
Arms; sitting quietly in the circle of men,
seldom talking with them, but showing a
spirit of nervous anxiety to hear all that was
said, and an uneasy readiness to join his
laughter with theirs over some rustic jest;
and he began to have his glass filled several
times, swallowing down its contents with
hasty gulps. He would go early to the inn,
and leave late; and the men said Matthew
had become a less cheerful companion, was
more chary of his words, and more ready to
quibble over what others said.

Neddy Kendal was always at the Garod
Arms, and he and Matthew often disagreed.
To some it seemed that it was the shoemaker
who provoked the blacksmith by unguarded
words, while there were others who said it

was Matthew who was generally in the wrong. To Matthew, however, each thing Neddy Kendal said, bore a double meaning which seemed to be pressing him by admissions and prevarications, gradually to his doom. But no one saw or understood this, saving Neddy Kendal and Matthew himself.

Nevertheless there was one gleam of happiness which broke through the dark cloud of his sorrow.

He was standing one afternoon in the smithy, a narrow bar of iron which he was trying to straighten in his hands, when he heard a footstep fall upon the threshold and tread lightly over the floor of the shop. He knew whose it was, for had he not listened to those feet as they made uncertainly toward him in early babyhood, and then with the dancing tread of childhood, and finally in the steadier step of youth and womanhood? He did not look up, however, but he listened intently and marked the fact that Maggie was making her way round the anvil, and that she paused within a yard of the place where he stood. Then, to his great joy, she spoke to him, timidly and hesitatingly, but with the old tenderness of tone.

"Mattha, old chap, we can't go on like this."

The bar of iron was thrown down and Matthew's hands laid on his sister's shoulders, and the two looked tearfully for a moment into each other's face.

"Mattha, we're friends, old chap?"

"Ay, my lass, we're friends, God knows! An' we'll be friends till death." And here Matthew's hands slipped from their resting-place until they reached those of his sister, and there was a warm, mutual hand-clasp, followed by a wringing of each other's hands which had in it something of the nature of an oath. And then they parted without a kiss or further word of explanation.

For days Maggie's heart had yearned toward her brother, and when she knew he was not looking, her eyes had followed him as he moved from place to place in the kitchen, or when sitting in front of the fire his gaze fixed upon the pages of a book which were never turned. The repulsion and horror which had been awakened in her that night when she stood for the first time face to face with the fact, that her brother was her lover's murderer, had gradually given way to a feeling of cold hatred. Then this frame of emotion slowly changed to one from which hate and love alike were banished; and in this mood she came by degrees to a knowledge of the truth, pity stealing with its softening influence into her heart as though fanned to her by angels' wings, until at last a warm full tide of affection rose within her, and she knew that what had been done—hateful, soul-scorching, though it was—had yet been done through love.

And then she sought the reconciliation for which both yearned.

Meanwhile, like a low murmuring accompaniment of minor chords, Maggie carried out quiet preparations for a plan that she had formed. She opened the painted chest of drawers that stood in her little bedroom, and lifting out the contents carefully smoothed them. Her summer dresses were to be folded and put away. The grey one with the pale pink spots—*he* had admired it and called it pretty, and that one—yes, she remembered him laying a bunch of wild roses against it, bidding her mark the harmony of colour. And then she caught her breath, and, resting her forehead on the edge of the open drawer, bit her lips to keep back the sobs which she could not repress, in spite of all her efforts. But she must not allow herself to give way; she had many things yet to do before the final carrying out of her plan, and so she turned once more to the contents of her drawer. There was the box which she kept in the corner—an old-fashioned wooden box, papered inside and out with a piece of wall-paper that had been given her by Mrs. Peacock; an odd scrap that had been left from the papering of one of the rooms at Derthwaite—this contained her treasures. Some of them she would take away with her—some which were of greater value than the rest. What a worthless collection it seemed ! A bit of blackened and crinkled maiden-hair, and the flower of an orchid dried and pressed out of shape; a letter, the only letter which Sidney Aschenburg had ever written to her ; a small round pincushion with a painted ship upon it, which Matthew had brought her once from the fair at Merton ; a pair of tiny morocco shoes which had belonged to the first doll she had ever had—the doll had long since been broken and destroyed ; a bundle of odds and ends of silk for patchings, and an old-fashioned purse worked in beads, with two lambs and very green trees on one side, and a house with a red roof and three blue beads, put at regular intervals to represent windows, on the other. This purse contained a small stock of half-sovereigns, which had come one by one to her on each birthday from Matthew. The maiden-hair and the orchid, the letter, the pincushion, and the purse were put together; the other things were returned to the box. Then she spread a large handkerchief on the floor and placed in it a change of linen, the treasures which were to go with her, and one or two other articles of clothing; after which she knotted up the corners and tied the whole into a secure bundle, putting it into one of the drawers where it was to await the execution of her plan.

Two nights after her reconciliation with Matthew, she sat white and sick at heart in the shadow of the broad mantel-shelf by the kitchen fire. Was the carrying out of her plan going to be beyond her strength, and was she going to die in making the attempt, she kept asking herself. And there came a convulsive spasm in her throat, and it seemed as if she must fight for breath. But she sat quietly, while loops of wool fell off her knitting-needles, and her fingers moved mechanically and bungled at her work.

To be gone from Staneby, gone where no one would recognize her, was her aim. To remain in her own village would be to court the gibes and sneers of those from whom she had in the old days held herself aloof—for Tom Farrar's wife was right in the main. Maggie had always been one who "kept herself to herself," and had let people know that the Tindales had their own pride. She recognized this fact, and yet curiously enough it took very little hold of her—she felt that it could be borne. It did not seem to her that it would have mattered much, had she to walk down the village with the whole of Staneby looking at her and crying shame. She did not think she would care. She had grown so tired, so cold, so indifferent; the weight of sorrow under which she laboured had benumbed her. It was a greater reason than this that was going to drive her from the shelter of her home.

To Maggie, thinking slowly and wearily, had come a train of thoughts which connected

itself closely with Matthew. Who would
answer the tongue of gossip clamouring to
know the name of her lover? Who could
point out a villager of Staneby, or any one
from an outlying hamlet, who had ever
stepped over the threshold of Jonathan Tindale's cottage as the wooer of his daughter?
Had it not been commonly said that Maggie
held her head above them all? And would
not the people talk this over amongst themselves, until at last they would agree that it
would be only likely that she who was so
proud would have had a gentleman for a
lover? Then, if a gentleman, would they not
look round and ask what gentleman it could
be? And surely to this question, or so it
seemed to Maggie, there could be but one
answer. Then, as light must follow darkness
and the full daylight upon the rising dawn,
so would the thoughts of all be turned backward to that mysterious death by drowning,
and the finding of the young owner of Derthwaite below the steep cliffs of the Devil's Pot.

And slowly, link by link, would the chain be formed. There would be somebody who would remember how just at that very time Matthew's face had been bruised and cut, and that he had kept closely to the smithy, and had not been seen for days in the village street or at the Garod Arms—perhaps even somebody might have seen him coming home from the Derthwaite woods on the fatal night; people always crowded up mysteriously and brought bit after bit of evidence, which, taken together, became as the witnesses of a crime. Moreover—and at this thought a thrill of terror would run through Maggie— had she not herself incriminated her brother by going up to Derthwaite and seeking an interview with Sidney? Would not the old servant who admitted her remember the impatience and distress which Maggie had shown when a doubt was expressed as to her being seen by the young master? Might not this fact be connected in the mind of the old nurse, with the birth of a child for whom no

father would be claimed? Besides, had not
Maggie, when leaving Sidney's room half-
frenzied with jealousy and despair, met her
rival, and made no attempt to hide from her
the reason of her presence at Derthwaite?
and would not this tall lady with the pale
face and sad eyes repeat the story that had
been told to her? And if so, would it
not agree bit by bit with other things,
until it would be found out how Matthew,
in his love and devotion, had avenged his
sister?

And upon this knowledge followed that of
an urgent necessity. She must leave her
home. She must loosen her hold upon all
that was dear to her ; must become a wanderer
upon the face of the earth ; must go forth as
though the mark of Cain was upon *her* brow ;
must do this and much more. She must lay
down her life, for is not the yielding up of
all we love the yielding up of our life—our
love is our life. She must give up her life,
lest she and her babe should become her

brother's accusers, and, rising up against him, be potent witnesses to his crime.

And so Maggie sat by the fireside knitting mechanically, the clicking of her needles and those of her mother making a monotonous kind of music. And the firelight flickered and leaped, throwing fantastic figures upon the walls and ceiling. It shone upon Mrs. Tindale's placid and rosy face; upon her cap, with its waving black ribbons; and upon her broad motherly bosom, and on the ample folds of her dress. How busily she knitted, rapidly changing the needles from hand to hand, and drawing off long lengths of wool from the ball which lay at her feet. And old Jonathan Tindale sat in the firelight too; and the arms of his chair glinted, and his twisted and toil-worn hands were thrown into sharp relief.

Nine o'clock struck with a thin shrill sound from the clock in the corner.

Another hour less to remain within the shelter of the old home. And the tightening about Maggie's heart increased, and her lips parted that she might take breath.

"Come, father," exclaimed Mrs. Tindale suddenly, as a vague kind of recollection dawned upon her of having heard the clock strike. "Isn't it time ye were in yer bed?"

It had come at last, and Maggie would have to bid good night and good-bye. '

"Good night," she said, still sitting in the shadow. "Good night, father; good night, mother." And the half-knitted sock slipped from her hands to the ground, and the room became dark, and there was a curious rushing sound in her ears, and it seemed as if she were falling, falling, falling; and then forgetfulness.

"Now, mind the step. Ye slipped as ye went up last night." Mrs. Tindale held the candle which she carried in her hand high above the old man's head, so that its light might fall uninterruptedly upon the stairs.

"I can mind mysel well enough," returned

old Jonathan querulously. "Ye might think I was blind an' decrapit, the way ye talk."

"Well, my feet go wrong wayses sometimes."

"Ay, yours. But then ye're clumsy, an' don't look where ye're goin'."

And so the two passed up the staircase and out of sight.

The falling had ceased, and Maggie had come to a resting-place, the confused rush gradually stilling itself in her ears, and the dark shadow rolling away from her eyes. She looked round the empty kitchen, not turning her head where it rested on the back of the chair, but moving her eyes slowly with a troubled, dazed expression. Was that horrible sickening feeling a dream, or was it death that had been near her? The next moment the mist of forgetfulness rolled from her brain, and she remembered all.

She remained seated a few minutes; and then placing her hands on her knees, rose with an effort to her feet. How the room

swam round with her! And how impossible
it was to stand erect without that firm grasp
upon the back of her mother's chair. It was
only by a great effort of will that she gradually
steadied her trembling limbs, breathing in a
careful, measured way as if to lessen the quick
beatings of her heart.

If she could only get upstairs before Matthew
came back, was the one definite thought which
took hold of her. She felt as if she could not
bear to see his face—could not endure the
familiar sound of his footsteps upon the
threshold. And the thought gave her
strength, and she went across the kitchen
toward the staircase, and so up to her little
room.

Everything that she would require had
already been laid out in readiness. There was
her hat and the long dark cloak, and the thick
knitted muffler which her mother had given
her the previous Christmas. The bundle was
yet in the drawer, but that was soon lifted out.
And beneath it was a letter written by Maggie

to her mother. This she placed on the dressing-
table, rearing it up against the speckled looking-glass, so that it would catch the eye of
any one coming into the room. It had been
carefully closed some days before, for Maggie
had no need to remind herself of its contents—
she knew them by heart. It had taken her a
long time to write that letter. It had been
difficult to find reasonable excuses for what she
was going to do ; and, having found them, to
put them in such a way that they should
neither create feelings of suspicion nor alarm.
She began by saying that it had long been her
wish to go into service, but that she had never
expressed it, fearing it might meet with her
parents' disapproval. Now, however, that she
had arrived at an age when it was desirable
that she should be making something for herself, and having seen several advertisements in
the Midland papers, she had determined upon
taking the necessary steps for leaving home
and going to seek personally for employment.
She said it would have been a great trouble to

her to have bidden them good-bye, and that,
after thinking the matter over carefully, she
intended to go away without any leave-taking,
believing that it would be the easiest for all. . . .
She hoped they would not think her unkind,
for the wish to act unkindly was far from her
thoughts. She would write soon to them, and
if she got a situation that suited her, she would
ask her mother to pack up and send off the
remainder of her clothes. But above all things
they were to keep up their hearts about her,
and not fidget themselves in any way. Would
they give her love to Bella Hind, and say she
was off to service, and would they say the same
to all inquiring friends? And then she added
an especial good-bye to her father, and her
mother, and Matthew.

Once in her room, Maggie neither hesitated
nor lingered over her final preparations ; but,
putting on cloak, hat, and muffler, took up her
bundle and seated herself on the edge of the
bed. She must wait until Matthew had come
in and the house was quiet.

Minute after minute passed, but so slowly that it seemed to Maggie she must have been sitting there for hours. And then the clock in the kitchen struck again with a thin, metallic, far-off ring, and Maggie knew that but one hour had gone by since she came upstairs. She dare not go till Matthew came in. For what if they met in the kitchen, or on the threshold, or upon the green? Would he not ask her where she was going at that time of night, and would he not detain her, nay, perhaps even forbid her going away at all?

Ah, there was the familiar footstep at last! And Maggie bent her head, eagerly listening to it. Yes, he had opened the door. And now he was walking across the kitchen. Would he sit down by the fire and have a pipe? No, that was a stupid thing to think of; he had never done that for—ah, how long it was! No, he would come straight up the stairs. Yes, she knew it. And now he was passing her door. And now he had opened his own.

Maggie buried her face in her hands, and as she did so, she began to tremble violently from head to foot. Could she go through with it? she again asked herself; could she carry out her plan?

The minutes passed slowly, until she heard another hour strike.

Eleven o'clock! Yes, she could go now. Faint and sick, she rose up and, taking her bundle, opened her door and stood listening with hearing that was preternaturally sharpened.

Only the ticking of the eight-day clock, faint by reason of its having to travel up the narrow twisting stair, could be heard. And Maggie stepped out upon the little landing, and with eyes turned in the darkness upon the door of her parents' room, stretched out empty hands toward it, and gave a silent catching of the breath that told of agony. One more step, and she was opposite the door of Matthew's room. With fingers that moved unhesitatingly, she laid her hand upon it, touching it lightly and lovingly. With blanched and trembling lips she kissed its panel, the silent catching of her breath growing into deep tearless sobs. Then she turned and went step by step down the stairs and across the kitchen, and so from beneath the roof of her father's house into the darkness and cold. Here she paused for fully a minute, and, with closed eyes and face that was pallid and drawn, let the east wind blow upon her.

Could the agony of death be greater than what she was suffering, she wondered?

But relief came, and tears ran down her cheeks. "Oh, Mattha, Mattha, old chap!" she said brokenly to herself between her sobs; "I lay down my life for ye. I go away that ye may live."

Strength came to her at last, and she went out into the darkness, her feet no longer helpless and stumbling, but gaining firmness with each step, the sentence ringing like a dirge upon her ears mingled with a tone of victory: "I go away that you may live."

CHAPTER III.

FLIGHT.

To look for the last time upon anything that has been familiar to us from childhood, will cause the whole of the past life lived in connection with it, to move like a shifting picture across the retina of the imagination : things that have been forgotten for years, will shape themselves and draw our hearts toward them with a vain yearning.

And so, as Maggie passed the last cottage in Staneby and came out upon the open road, the sight of the hedges, the trees, the fields on either side, nay, each gateway leading into them, stirred up in her benumbed brain the quickening tide of life. The emotion was

painful, but its very painfulness seemed to
have the power of deadening for a while
that other and greater agony under which
she suffered. There was the field, in which
Matthew used to take her when a little
child to gather the cowslips, which later he
made into balls for her to play with. She
could remember the scent of the cowslips,
and their warmth as, gathered in the sunshine,
she would lay them against her cheek. Oh,
what sweet days! The recollection of their
babyish trials and sorrows had passed from
her; she could remember nothing but their
peacefulness, Matthew filling up her world;
her guardian, her playfellow. And here, just
beside this gateway, were the two boulders
still standing, one higher than the other, but
both looking dwarfed in comparison with her
childish ideas of them, just as in the days
when she would play at being queen, and
Matthew, to please her, at being king. How
she had always insisted upon sitting on the
higher stone, and having the largest branch

of hawthorn; for each carried branches as
sceptres, and wore upon their heads wreaths
of daisies for crowns. A mournful pang of
regret shot through Maggie's heart as she
called to mind this piece of childish selfishness.
How she wished she had always sat on the
lower stone and had given up the more
splendid sceptre! Then, as she took the next
turn in the road, and came to that part of it
where, when the common-lands had been
enclosed, a rough waste bit had been left
with lavish negligence on either side, a vision
of sunny days and light breezes rose before
her, and she saw upon one of the banks a
little child listening with rapturous attention
to a story which was being told to her—
a story which was only told when sitting on
that bank, and to which she was never tired
of listening until the two had become insepar-
able in her mind—the bank, with its growth
of wild thyme and rock-roses, and the sound
of Matthew's voice as he told of the man
who was shipwrecked and who fell asleep on

the shore, and who awoke to find that he had been fastened down to the ground by the hands of tiny men. And as Maggie passed that bank in the starlight, a strong wish seized her to gather a bit of the wild thyme and some of the yellow rock-roses, and she made a momentary pause, intending to turn off the road to carry out her wish. But a sudden blast of east wind recalled to her the fact that November was no month for flowers, and she went on again, wondering to herself that, in spite of all she was enduring, this disappointment, trivial though it seemed, had yet the power to sting.

After a time the road began to grow less familiar, and there were fewer things to be remembered. She passed an oak tree which had been struck by lightning some summers previously—this tree only a few minutes before had afforded her father shelter from the storm—and she shuddered as she asked herself, whether it would not have been better for the old man thus to have met his death, than to have lived only to learn, perhaps, at last of the disgrace which had befallen both his children. And after this, the trees and hedge-rows became as things that have been rarely seen; not wholly unrecognizable and yet not wholly familiar; until at length, as she walked on, they grew strange to her, and the visions of her childhood faded, leaving the agony of parting from her home and those who alone were dear to her on earth, together with the stern realities of her position, to fill her heart.

It seemed to her that she must have been walking for at least two hours; her limbs were aching and tremulous, and she was beginning to feel sorely in need of rest. She had passed several cottages, but there had been no light in the windows. Had there been lights, however, she dared not have knocked and asked for admittance, for she would not risk doing anything by which the road she had taken might be traced. Yet to go on much further she knew to be im-

possible. If only she could find an outhouse
that would shelter her from the wind! And
with this thought in her mind, she paused
occasionally and peered over the wall or hedge
by which the road was skirted into the fields
beyond. At last a haystack loomed out of
the darkness, huge, rotund, and slightly heel-
ing over to one side, which offered promise
of shelter. To go through a gate near, and
then to mount the railing by which the stack
was enclosed, was the work of a few minutes.
Carefully did she feel her way round, coming
at last to a triangular opening where a portion
of the hay had been cut and carried away
for fodder, and which opened from the ground
skywards. At the bottom of this opening
lay a quantity of loose hay which could be
used both for bed and covering. No sooner
did she see this, than, with a sob of utter
weariness, she threw herself down amongst
it; putting a sufficient quantity beneath her
head for a pillow, and loosely scattering the
rest above her where she lay. What would

her mother say, she thought, could she have seen her child lying like that beneath the open starlight? And then in a few moments she forgot the loneliness of her position, her sorrows, and her fears, and was sleeping dreamlessly.

It was yet starlight when she awoke, but a pale radiance in the east had begun to spread faintly towards the zenith. For a minute she could not understand where she was, and the cramping of her limbs and their aching and stiffness puzzled her. Then the events of the past night flashed upon her, and she fell back with closed eyes against the wall of hay. Could she go on, she wondered? Would she have strength to walk so many miles? Then, as she remembered how important to Matthew was the success of her undertaking, how great the need for her to be securely hidden from the prying eyes of Staneby, courage and strength came slowly back. Again she raised herself upon the soft yielding mass, and, taking off her hat, smoothed her hair a little and fastened up the heavy braids; after which, stiff and cramped though she was, she rose to her feet, shaking off the loose bits of hay from her dress and re-arranging its folds.

She wanted to get still some miles farther from Staneby, before the sun was up and other pedestrians were upon the road; and wondering what time it was, she looked at the line of hills where the faint radiance showed the point at which the sun would presently show itself. But it told her nothing of the hour of the morning; for the appearance of the heavens could never stand to her, as it stood to her brother, in the place of the old eight-day clock at home.

She wanted to take the train at Thirldale, a place fifteen miles south of Merton, thinking that it would be less likely that she should be recognized there than in the town so near Staneby. It seemed scarcely probable to her that she could have got more than nine or ten miles on the road to Thirldale; and as she thought of the five or six miles that yet were to be traversed before she could reach it, her heart failed her again, and it was only by an effort that she prevented herself from sinking, in weariness of mind and body, to the ground. If only she could see a cart or conveyance of any kind going in the same direction, she would beg for a seat, was the thought by which she strove to encourage herself; forgetting how, but a few minutes before, her sole desire had been to accomplish the remainder of her journey while it was too early for her to meet any one on the road.

And then once again she set off, feeling how vast a place is the world to one who, saving the desire to put leagues between herself and her home, is without end or aim. The road on which she walked was an ever endless track, which, though winding, yet stretched into the vast wilderness of unknown countries. It would lead her past villages and towns; nevertheless only in those a long way off could she find rest. But would it indeed be rest even in those distant places, with the faces of strangers round her, and the memory of a far-off village in her heart? Ah, me! Then, as a child will turn its aching head toward the bosom of its mother, so did Maggie's thoughts go back to those summer evenings when, with the hope of meeting Sidney Aschenburg, life's cup of joy was full. She felt the touch of his caressing finger on her cheek; she saw the expression of admiration in his eyes ere he stooped to kiss her, and words that had sent the blood in fleeting waves across her cheeks sounded once more clearly and distinctly upon her ear. But the respite was only momentary, and the tasting of past joys made the bitterness of the lees she was drinking the more bitter.

Maggie walked on steadily in the keen wind, the faint light in the east spreading higher up the heavens and further upon each side of the horizon. The birds were beginning to stir in the hedges, and occasionally a little

feathered creature would fly as if half awake
across the road, while a hare would come with
long bounding leaps, to pause so soon as it
came in sight of her, and then, turning, dash
back at full speed the way it came. Once
she passed the outskirts of a village, and
there she saw the smoke rising from several
chimneys; but, though hungry and faint for
want of food, she did not stop and ask for
anything to eat, the village seeming to her
tortured fancy to be still too near to Staneby.
It was at this place she heard the clock strike
six. Her mother would have got the fire
lighted at home, and would be busy downstairs wondering why she did not come. And
then, because Maggie sometimes overslept herself, and the mother would not have her
child disturbed, Maggie could see her moving
carefully, taking the cup of tea to the old
man who would still be in bed, treading
lightly, and guarding the cup and saucer lest
they should rattle as she passed her child's
door. And Maggie's hands closed tightly, her

pale lips pressing themselves firmly one upon the other, while she gave one swift, wild look, such as a hunted animal might give, round the distant horizon. But she still walked on.

Then there came a toilsome hill, and presently a long, straight road; then a piece of waste land enclosed by moss-covered walls; again another hill closed in by hedges and trees, until at length it seemed to Maggie as if she must faint. If only some cart or waggon would pass her way! And she turned her eyes back longingly, for by this time the light had spread more and more, and she could see every object clearly in the valley.

Was it fancy, or was there something making its way slowly down one of the hilly bits of road? Maggie shaded her eyes, and looked long and fixedly. Certainly it moved; but whether it was anything likely to be able to afford her help, Maggie could not tell. The sense of weariness was creeping over her, however, so overwhelmingly, that she felt, no

matter what that slowly moving object might
be, she must sit down and wait for it.

Nearer and nearer it came—a spring cart
with a seat across it, upon which sat a broad-
shouldered, middle-aged, comely man in grey
frieze overcoat and cap with fur-lined lappets
tied down above his ears. He looked curiously
at Maggie when she rose from the heap of
stones, upon which she had been resting, at
the side of the road and came toward him.

"What do ye say? I'se rather hard o'
hearin'," he shouted to something which she
had said. Then, upon her repeating it in a
louder tone, he told her he was on his way to
Thirldale, and that if she were going there
she might get in, and he would give her a
ride, for he reckoned two would be as light
for the old horse to carry as one.

"Thank you," returned Maggie, climbing up
as he directed her, by the wheel into the cart,
too tired to feel shy or frightened.

"Where are ye goin'?" asked the man, more
from a desire to appear sociable than from any

feeling of curiosity, while he shook the reins
as a sign to the old horse that it might
go on.

"I don't know." And Maggie felt frightened, wondering if he could possibly have
heard that she had run away from Staneby.

"Ye don't know! Why, that's a queer
job."

"I mean it all depends on the train."

"The train! Why, are ye goin' to get
head-fust into any that comes up?" shouted
the man in a good-natured kind of way, looking round at his companion as he spoke.
Then, seeing the dark circles round the girl's
eyes and the pallor of her cheeks, his thoughts
were diverted, and he asked her if she had
come far, for she looked "a bit weary."

"Yes; I've been walkin' for days an' days."
The words, though literally untrue—and
Maggie knew it—nevertheless appeared to
her less untrue than the actual truth would
have been, so many hours did it seem since
she had left her home.

"An' ye don't seem over strong either. My lasses would make two o' ye, I reckon."

"Oh, but I'm quite strong." And the speaker's cheeks flushed painfully. "I'm only tired because I've not had any breakfast.' Then she added hurriedly, as though this required an explanation, "I was afraid of missing the train, ye know, if I stopped to get any."

The man turned his head and looked at his horse, shaking the reins from time to time, while he cogitated upon something that evidently required the whole power of his mind. At length he looked round at Maggie, and put a hand into one of his greatcoat pockets. "I've been just askin' myself whether ye'd be above eatin' some bread-an'-cheese that my missis put up in a han'kercher for me afore I left home. Ye see, I carry 'baccy in my pockets, an' all mak o' things; but if ye're not ower partic'lar, an' don't mind the smell of a pipe—— "

Maggie lifted up her face with a melancholy

smile as the man paused. She had known the day when such fare as was being offered her, would have been rejected with something like disgust; now, however, it could only be accepted thankfully.

"Ye'll hev it? Well, that's something like." And the man's rosy face beamed with satisfaction. "Open it out, an' don't spare it; there's plenty for me where that comes from."

Maggie, thus urged, ate the bread and cheese, and not without relish, for youth is vigorous, and its appetite persistently strong. By the time the last piece had been swallowed, she was beginning to feel refreshed, and a faint colour had come into her lips and cheeks.

"Now then, we only want a drop o' milk or tea, an' ye wad hev had a grand breakfast." The countryman said this with a chuckle, as though extremely delighted with the part which he had played, and his face beamed.

"I thank ye kindly, I'm sure," returned Maggie, something of her natural shyness coming back, as a quickened vitality stole through her frame.

"Not a bit, not a bit, my lass. Never say a word about it," shouted the man with considerable emphasis, and in great good humour with himself, as he turned his attention outwardly upon his horse, shaking the reins, and laying his walking-stick across its back with considerable energy.

By this time the sun had cleared the bank of cloud which rested on the top of the hills, and was shining with bright cold gleams down the valley. The wind had fallen, and a growing mildness in the air indicated that a change might be looked for.

"We'll hev rain afore night," remarked Maggie's benefactor, giving an energetic sweep with his stick, that embraced at least three points of the compass. "But I suppose ye'll be away from these parts."

The last words, though spoken so loud and
cheerily, fell with the weight of lead upon
Maggie. " Away from these parts."   Four
simple words, but what did they not mean
to her ? She lifted up shy, frightened eyes,
and made no reply, but looked over the
unfamiliar landscape with a vague yearning.
She had never been further from home than
Merton, where she would go on market days
with her mother ; and twice to Thirldale, when
Matthew had taken her to the fair.   And
now that she was quite away from the familiar
landmarks—even the Pennine range had
changed its shape, and no longer bore any
resemblance to the hills she knew—she was
getting nervous and frightened ; a fuller sense
of her desolateness than any hitherto borne in
upon her, was stealing with cold hands round
her heart.   She had begun to grow accustomed
to the voice of the burly countryman and his
rough, though kindly ways, and, without being
aware of it, she already clung instinctively to
him, and felt a sense of protection from his

presence; but even this poor source of comfort
fell away with his words.

"How far are we from Thirldale?" she
asked, with an inward shrinking at the
prospect of losing the old countryman's protection.

"There, look ye. Past them trees. Now
then—down the handle o' my stick—ay,
that's right—no, cast yer eyes a bit this way.
D' ye see them chimlas (chimneys)?"

Maggie was obliged to confess she did.

A few minutes after, her companion drew up
the old horse, and, pointing to a lane, told
her that, if she would go down it, she would
find it was a near way to the station; he
would have been glad to have driven her
there himself, up to the very doors, but
business taking him into the lower part of the
town, he could not easily spare the time which
such extension of his journey would necessi-
tate. Then, after helping her out of the cart,
he shook his stick cheerfully at her, and wished
her good day and good luck. So they parted.

Maggie knew several of the manufacturing towns by name. But they were all alike to her; all wonderfully big places, lying probably at equal distances from Staneby, in far unknown counties. There could be no difference, she thought, between them; one would be as good as another to hide in. She would like to have gone to the largest, could she have distinguished it, because it was only natural to suppose that the larger the town, the greater abundance of work and the more easy to find it. But as this could not be done, she fixed at random in her own mind upon one of them, and it was the name of this town she gave when she got to the station and asked for a ticket. She was disconcerted to find how much money it cost; but she was too shy to ask the clerk if he would take it back and give her another to some place not quite so far off. On the platform she found a sprinkling of people, and was glad to go to the further end, where she saw an isolated seat. She had been told that a train would be up in a few minutes, which would take her to her destination; but it seemed to her a long time before it actually arrived, and she was hustled into an empty compartment. Quickly to her did the train start, and feeling that the last link with her home was broken and all need for self-control gone, she began to weep unrestrainedly.

Past hedges, trees, houses, broad open fields, and patches of woodland ; the telegraph wires rising and falling steadily ; the white steam of the engine now obscuring the view ; now, floating above the tops of the carriages, melting away as piles of softest down upon the breeze. Wayside stations appeared for a few second as a band of light colouring ; and then the hedges, the woods and fields. Then cuttings again, and once a tunnel into which the train rushed with a shrill whistle, the darkness and muffled roar being exchanged in a few minutes for the full daylight and the sound of monotonously playing wheels. And the train heeled gently and steadily, sometimes toward one side, sometimes toward the other, as it rounded the curves; then it rushed forward on the lengths of level road, until it came into a flat country, with scant vegetation and trees of stunted growth. The weather had changed, the sun no longer shone, and the atmosphere had become thick and murky. Tall chimneys began to appear, and from some of them were pouring volumes of smoke; now streets of brick houses, and huge factories and workshops with the names of their owners written along their length.

Maggie had given up crying, and had begun to look at this strange town which she was approaching, so unlike Merton or Thirldale with their clean streets and houses newly coloured or painted every year. It must be the place to which she intended going, she thought; it looked so large. As she gazed down into the narrow streets, above which the train was running, their squalor and dingy uniformity appalled her. Surely no work could be had there, she thought to herself; there

could only be struggling and fighting amongst
the people for daily bread. But the train
ran by the side of a high wall and the view
was shut out, and in another minute a gloomy
station was entered and the engine came to a
standstill. Maggie got up hurriedly, feeling
afraid of being carried past her destination.
But before she had opened the door of her
compartment, a porter impatiently told her to
sit down again, for she would have to travel
fifty or sixty miles before she could reach the
place she named to him. It was a relief to be
told this, for those dingy streets had filled her
with dread.

The engine was soon again on the move,
and Maggie sat leaning forward to watch the
landscape flying past her.

It was mid-day when she stepped out of the
train, feeling confused and frightened by the
noise of the busy station, its crowds of pas-
sengers and its officials hurrying to and fro.
Where should she go? And as she asked herself this question, she looked round helplessly

at the passers-by. But most of them were too much occupied to notice her; and others, if they looked at all, gave but a passing glance, the few only having time to look and look again at the rare loveliness of her face, while they wondered that she should stand there with arms folded upon her bundle, and make no effort to step into a carriage or move away. Perhaps she was waiting for some one; and then those who had leisure enough for this thought also passed on. In a little while the train started again, and the once busy platform became deserted, saving for a few porters, whose looks, directed curiously upon Maggie, roused her to a sense of the conspicuousness of her position. She had seen a continuous stream of people making its way through a large doorway, so she too turned her steps in that direction, and was soon outside the station and in a busy street.

Feeling forlorn and helpless, she set off walking aimlessly. First down one street and then up another, until she got into a poorer part of the town; but still amongst streets that were without the squalor of those she had seen from the train, and whose dinginess was often relieved by a flower-pot in a window, or by a table with a cloth over it, or by some such attempt at colour and brightness. Maggie was looking only for some place that would afford her a temporary shelter. She wanted to have time to think quietly upon all she had come through, and to give herself that rest of which she stood so sorely in need. At last, in a house smaller than those immediately about it, but clean-looking and respectable, she saw a card setting forth that a good bed was to be had within; and, after knocking at the door and asking if she could have shelter for one night, she stepped over the threshold, a faint sense of relief coming to her with the thought that, for a few hours at least, her wanderings might end.

CHAPTER IV.

STRUGGLES.

WEARY and exhausted, Maggie allowed herself a respite from all thought connected with the practical one of the means whereby she was to obtain a livelihood; on the morrow, she told herself, she would try to carry into execution the plans roughly formed at Staneby; she would find out the names of some of the great shops and go and ask for work. Work would be sure to be easily got by one who was a good sewer; and that she was a good needlewoman Maggie knew. So, on the day following that on which she had come to the great city, when she went downstairs into the room that was half kitchen, half parlour, which for the time she occupied with her landlady, she began to make inquiries as to the houses from which employment might be obtained.

" You'll fin' these big 'ouses 'ave more people than they've work for," returned the owner of the house in answer, seating herself at the table opposite to Maggie. She was a hard-featured, middle-aged woman; rather big and bony, with a hollow chest, and an asthmatic difficulty in her breathing.

" Well, if you think so, I would be quite willing to try the smaller ones." Maggie was so confident in her powers of sewing, and so full of belief in the quantity of work which must necessarily be only waiting for the hands that were willing to do it, that she felt nothing daunted by the woman's words.

" What put it in your 'ead to come 'ere ? People would do better for themselves if they would stay at their own country 'omes."

" I've long wanted to make something for myself."

"Then why not 'ave gone into service? You're a likely looking young woman."

"I did not care about it." Maggie's pale face flushed a little and she stooped hurriedly over her teacup.

The woman looked suspiciously at her, and for several minutes there was no sound but that of the laboured breathing.

"I 'ope you've not been in any trouble?"

Maggie started, and the beautiful soft eyes looked up with an expression of sudden fear.

"I'm not one for 'aving trouble brought to me. My lodgings is respectable. If there's anything be'ind the scenes you'd better name it." The woman's face hardened as she spoke.

Poor Maggie! She sat looking helplessly at her interrogator, feeling as if the very chair beneath her would slide away. But there was no rush of colour to her cheeks; nor, on the other hand, was there an increase of pallor or whitening of the lips.

Seeing that Maggie was making no attempt to reply, the woman told her she "had better name it," in a tone that seemed to say the speaker was too sharp and shrewd for it to be possible that she could ever be deceived.

Maggie moved uneasily on her chair, while her eyes slowly filled with tears. Then she said, but not without effort, " You are quite right. I'm in great trouble."

" Then if that's the case I'll thank you to take yourself off. You can finish your break-fast. Nobody can ever say of me that I'm 'ard. I look after myself, that's all."

These words were listened to with a sub-mission which was coupled with the apathy of despair. Maggie felt she had deceived them at home ; she had indirectly led Matthew into doing—ah, what had he not done! Could she therefore rebel against the edict of this woman ?

But when the door of the house was closed upon her and she had gone out carrying her bundle into the street, something like the blank feeling of desolation seized upon her which she had felt when leaving Stanchy.

There was no threshold over which she might step; no roof beneath which she might close her eyes in untroubled sleep. The long unending road had lost itself in the labyrinths of a city; that was the only difference; the strangeness and desolation were the same.

Maggie's thoughts wandered back to her girlhood, to that time when she had neither spoken to Sidney Aschenburg, nor thought of speaking to him.

How peaceful was that pleasant vista of life! There were the changes of seasons, the changes of day and night; in all else it had been undisturbed. And yet how little had she valued its peacefulness! To sit on the doorstep at home in the long summer afternoons, her knitting in her hand, had been but a part of the day's work. What would she not have given now to be able to do it? She had done it as regularly as she washed the breakfast things, dusted the brass candlesticks and the china dogs on the mantel-shelf; and now, on looking back, she saw how balmy the air had been, how comfortable and warm the sunshine, and how the monotonous click, click of her needles had been as the singing of a lullaby which had hushed her into a dreaminess that was half wakefulness, half sleep. And she remembered the sounds that used to come to her from the smithy ; the faint clanking of a chain perhaps, or the sharp ring of iron, the soft sound of the bellows, followed by the clash, clash of the hammers as Matthew and her father shaped some piece of work upon the anvil. Next came the remembrance of the familiar burr of the old clock as it struck four. She had always been rather sorry to hear it ; for by that time she had sat so long on the doorstep that the dreaminess of mood induced by her own occupation and the sounds which had been around her, had worked a lethargic kind of spell upon her brain. She had run the knitting needles into her ball of wool and had got up, going out of the full blaze of the sunshine into the yet sunny kitchen. And, ah ! how well she could recall it all ! The soft singing of the kettle where it hung upon a crook over the fire; the smell, perhaps, of a pasty that was baking in the oven, or of oatcake that was being browned on the bars. And presently, the sound of the heavy quick tread of her mother coming in at the door.

Maggie could get no further. Looking down the ugly street, she drew her next breath with a catching noise and drove her heels firmly against the pavement. Would these pictures be for ever coming to her? she asked herself.

The lodging-house keeper had been right. Whenever Maggie summoned courage to go into a large shop to ask for work, she was told they had no sewing done out of their own establishment, or that they had their own people whom they regularly employed, or if she went to such and such a place she would probably get what she wanted; these were amongst the courteous answers she received. But there were many others who told the same things in roughly spoken tones and with impatient gestures. It was past midday, and

she began to try the smaller shops. The
result, however, was the same; there was
little work, she was told, and far too many
workers. Sick at heart and physically exhausted, it seemed to her as if the maze of
streets and shops would never end, and that
she was always to go on asking and always
to go on being refused, and yet to still keep
on walking and trying to get work. Down
broad streets filled with carriages and fashionable ladies, and beautiful shop windows
such as she had never seen the like, even
when the shopkeepers at Merton decked
their windows for Christmas; then into
narrower ones where few carriages went and
fine ladies were never seen, until she came
where there were only slums and alleys.
From these she turned away hurriedly, and
worked back, in a way unknown to herself,
into the fine grand streets. But by-and-
by she began to walk mechanically, and forgot to look for the shop windows, which,
when filled with beautifully stitched under-

clothing, had been to her as a sign that she might go and ask for work within. Indeed, she had ceased to think of them. She had ceased, in fact, to think of anything saving to wonder in a benumbed sort of way for how many hours longer she could walk. She must not faint in the streets, she kept telling herself; people would pick her up and carry her perhaps to a police-station, and there they would make her give up her name. And if she once told it to anybody, even in this great city, she would always be afraid, and would feel that at any moment Matthew, or her father or mother, might be coming to find her and take her home. But her limbs were beginning to tremble under her; and her sight failed at times as though a dark cloud came over it, making the figures of the passers-by invisible. And yet she still walked on.

Presently, a light wind arose which played about her face, bringing a sense of refreshment and a consciousness that the air was clearer and more country-like. So

instead of looking with half-lowered eyelids directly on the footpath before her, she
lifted up her head a little. She had got to
the outskirts of the town. A row of small
brick houses stood on either side of the street ;
and beyond these were a few cottages irregu-
larly built, and of a much older date than
the small houses ; and further still a grimy-
looking bit of common, blocked in by a railway embankment, which was pierced in
several places by archways. As she looked
at these things a faint interest was aroused
in her, and she was pleased to see that she
had come to the end of the shops and houses.
But if the houses and shops had ceased, her
walking must also cease. It would be of no
use to go out into the country. Besides, she
wanted food, and there was no food to be
found in open fields ; and she was afraid of
going into villages, it would be so easy for
the people in them to find out about her and
tell of her. No, she had better stay in the
town, if possible.

She glanced at the brick houses, but there was something in their sameness and neat primness which made her feel she could not knock at any of their doors and ask for lodgings. Besides, even if any of them took in lodgers, she felt sure they would ask more money than she could possibly give; for already the store of half-sovereigns, which had seemed large in Maggie's eyes, had diminished so seriously—and this was but the second day since she had left Staneby and as yet had found no work—that she foresaw the necessity of going into a much humbler lodging than that which had sheltered her the previous night. She must try if she could find any one who would take her in at one of the cottages.

"No, we don't take no lodgers," was the first answer she received, and the door of the cottage was slammed in her face. She was growing accustomed to rebuffs, and took this one quietly. A narrow slip of garden divided the next one from the road. It was a larger cottage than the others, and had more windows in it, and the door had lately had a coat of paint. She hesitated, therefore, before she unlatched the low wicket. Perhaps the people here would slam the door and let her see that they considered her question insulting. But Maggie's need was great, and with great needs we grow less scrupulous. So she unfastened the latch, and going up the path, which was made of cinders, broken pots, and other refuse, she knocked at the door. She could hear some one moving about inside, and presently the door was opened.

"No, I can't say that we ever take in lodgers," hesitatingly answered a young fair-haired woman with a baby in her arms. "I think you would be more likely to get what you want further in the town."

But Maggie did not want that; she did not want to go back into the maze of bewildering streets. Besides, her strength was well-nigh spent, and she knew if she tried to walk much further she must fall exhausted. So, because this woman had not roughly silenced her, and being, moreover, young—scarcely more than three or four years Maggie's senior—it did not seem very difficult to follow up the first question by another, which had in it something of persuasiveness.

"Well, I don't know what to say about it, I'm sure," again returned the woman of the cottage, speaking pleasantly, though still showing her hesitation. "You see, I would hardly like to promise anything till I've seen my husband, and he doesn't come home from his work till after six."

"I could wait," pleaded Maggie. She had learned since the morning to be more persistent. "I could sit for a bit here on the doorstep, if I might."

"Nay, nay; I can do better for you than that, anyway." The woman's voice was reassuring, and she smiled at Maggie. "I can ask you in, if I don't like to make arrangements about anything strange till Tom comes in."

The warmth and cheerfulness of the kitchen into which Maggie was led, and the gentle friendliness of the woman, did what neither the blank strangeness of the streets nor the rough answers of the shopkeepers had the power to do ; and as the woman drew a chair in front of the fire, and motioned to her to be seated, Maggie's fortitude gave way, and sinking down upon it, she began to tremble violently from head to foot, and broke into a fit of uncontrollable weeping.

"Oh, dear me! Whatever is the matter? Is it trouble of some kind, or are you ill?" The woman, though startled, was speaking very gently, and laid her disengaged hand— for she still carried her baby—with a sympathetic touch on Maggie's shoulder.

But Maggie, though she had been accustomed to be petted and kindly treated all her life, could only weep the more bitterly, so strangely did this woman's kindness affect her.

"I'll tell you what—I'll make you a cup of tea. Whenever I feel a bit upset, or overdone

—and I wasn't very strong for a good bit after baby came—I find there's nothing that cheers me so well. And look you, the kettle's boiling, so that it will not be many minutes before it's ready."

So saying, the woman laid her baby down in a cradle that was standing near the fire, carrying on her preparations for tea-making, while she kept up a running string of sentences that were soothing and cheerful by turns, and which never required any answers; until at last Maggie recovered herself a little, and began to apologize to her entertainer.

" Oh, never such a thing ! Why, you needn't ask my pardon." And the courtesy of the woman's nature caused her to make a pretty deprecatory gesture with her hands. " If you've been seeking work all day, I'm sure you must be tired enough."

" I never thought it would be so bad to get." And as Maggie looked up, the expression of her face plainly showed how well this new lesson had been learned.

"It's a hard fight amongst some of them, I can tell you." The woman, well contented in her home, her husband and child, shook her head pityingly.

"A hard fight," echoed Maggie, in a sad voice; but she was not thinking of those of whom the woman had spoken, but of herself.

After this, the woman took her baby in her arms again, and sat down on the other side of the small tea-table which she had placed near Maggie, slowly swaying herself from side to side, as the little one refused to be sent to sleep. Then, by way of finding amusement for her visitor, she began to tell in her cheery, pleasant voice of how she had been brought up in the country, but had always had a fancy for going into service in a large town; and then the clergyman's wife in the parish in which she lived hearing of a situation suitable for her, she had come and lived in it for two years, when, after being engaged to Tom for the greater part of that time, she had given up her place and had married. And the

woman told Maggie her name—Mary Kesteven
she said it was, and Mary Kenerdy before she
was married—and the name of the village
where she had lived as a girl.

Maggie listened quietly to all that the rosy,
bright-eyed little mother was saying, drinking
the tea that had been poured out for her, and
from time to time lifting a piece of bread-and-
butter to her lips.   She felt that she was
acting in a churlish way by making no
response to these confidences; but how could
it have been possible for her to tell her tale?

"I suppose you are from the country?"
asked Mary Kesteven presently.

"Yes, I'm from the country."

Mary had seen that the question had not
been a pleasant one to her visitor, so she
changed the subject.   But she kept wondering all the same why the girl had left the
country without the certainty of a situation
or work.   Presently, however, they broke
the silence and talked for awhile on indifferent subjects, Maggie being preoccupied

and occasionally answering so much at random as to startle her hearer. At last the twilight quite closed in upon the little kitchen, and Maggie said abruptly—

"My home is a long way from here. I don't want to talk much about it, because we've had a deal o' trouble. But you can call me Maggie if you like, for that is my name."

"I like Maggie. It's a name we've favoured a deal in our family," returned Mary, her native courtesy again causing her to comment upon that part of her visitor's communication which seemed least likely to give pain. But the wonder only grew the stronger within her, as to what could have sent this pretty, sad-faced young woman into a great town for work, with not a person in it whom she knew.

A little while longer they talked, but about Mary's affairs only; the baby, and about the difficulty they had in choosing a name for her, the father wanting Keziah because it

had been his mother's, while she, Mary, dis-
liked it and had at last persuaded him into
having it called Annie after his sister, telling
him that Keziah and Kesteven sounded too
much the same to go well together. From
this she went on to tell Maggie how much
heavier the baby had grown in the last month;
not that she had weighed it, because that
would have been unlucky, but because she
knew by carrying it and by the depth of
the impression it made in its little feather
bed. She wondered how long it would be
before it could walk, and she asked Maggie
if she knew about such things. And Maggie's
eyes dropped suddenly, and Mary thought
there was a change in her colour—but it
might have been the rosy flickering of the
firelight upon her cheeks. Mary then told
of the steady husband she had got; and of
the wages brought home on the Saturday
nights; and of the money they were trying
to put away in a bank. And here the tread
of a man's foot upon the cinder path outside

caused Mary to pause, and after listening for a moment, she said, " Yes, it's Tom. I do hope he'll let me have you for a lodger, for when he's at work I feel lonesome at times."

A short, squarely built man opened the door, pausing for a moment on the threshold when he saw that the hearth was occupied by two people. Then he stamped his feet and came in with a sonorous cough. He was a dark man, with a closely cut black beard, and eyes that were set rather widely apart.

" This young person has been inquiring for lodgings," began Mary at once. " And she called here to ask if we took in anybody."

" What do you say ? " And the man flung his hat down impatiently, coming forward into the firelight.

" I said—— " But the wife got no further, hesitating and looking up with a surprised expression as she began once more to sway herself backward and forward, the man's entrance having disturbed the child. Then she asked abruptly, " Has something gone wrong ? "

" Yes, there's the very devil's game to play. It's who'll be the strongest—the men with the money or us. I told you it would come to it. We've gone out on strike."

The man spoke in an angry, half-sulky tone, and threw himself into a chair, never so much as casting his eyes on the stranger who was seated at his hearth.

" What will it mean to us ? " and the hand of the mother softly patted the back of her child, while she looked across anxiously at her husband.

" Mean ! Why, it means there will be no work and no wages until one of us gives in. I tell you it'll be a fight as to who'll be strongest."

" Didn't you want to go out ? "

" I—no. I was fairly well satisfied. But the other chaps would have torn the life out o' me if I'd said a word."

" Well, it's a good job we've got our savings."

"Oh, be hanged to the savings! We didn't put them by, just to spend in this way."

There was silence for a few minutes, during which the man stared resentfully at the fire.

"What do you think if I take in this young person as lodger?" presently asked Mary in her quiet voice. "If I can be making something, even if it is ever so little, while you're out o' work, it will be better than if I was doing nothing."

The man turned his head slowly and looked at his wife, and then from his wife to Maggie.

"She's been here a good bit of the afternoon, and we've had a long talk together," continued Mary. "She's come to seek for work."

"Yes, I want work." And Maggie met the man's steady gaze with a composed, if sad expression.

"Settle it between you"—and here the man looked back at his wife—"I'm so badly put about I can only think of my own affairs."

So Maggie became a lodger with the Kestevens.

But no work could be found. Each day Maggie put on her hat and long dark cloak, and went again and yet again into the gloomy streets with the same request upon her lips. Some one must do the sewing, she kept saying to herself; all the beautiful tucks and frills could not come by chance into the piles of garments; and, if some one did them, why should she not be employed in this work? At last her courage failed, and with it her strength, and she told Mary that she must give up trying to look for work, and that if nothing came to her she must go home. But she did not mean to go home; it was only her way of telling Mary that she would have to leave her.

And Mary sat that evening for a whole hour silent by the fireside, her fingers moving very slowly over the little garment she was making, while her thoughts were busy upon a plan that had come into her mind. There were difficulties evidently about it, for her brow puckered itself up into lines

every now and again. At last she rolled up
her work, saying abruptly to Maggie that if
she would go with her on the following
morning they would see what could be done
by a united effort. So the next day Mary
took her to the house in the large fashionable
square where she had lived as servant. And
when Mary had sent up her name the two
were shown into the morning-room, where
four fair-haired girls, with pleasant smiles and
bright, vivacious ways of talking, were seated.
Then Mary told how the young person who
was with her had come up from the country,
and was wanting to support herself by her
needle ; and how she could do open-hemming,
gathering, felling, and feather-stitching, better
almost than any one whom she had ever seen ;
and if the young ladies would permit such
a thing, Maggie could show some specimens
of her work, so that they might judge of it
for themselves. And the four fair heads
stooped over the specimens, and the young
voices commended and praised, to Mary's

and Maggie's full content. Then low-toned
conversations and whisperings passed between
the sisters, followed by confidential nods; and
then an offer was made to Maggie which
seemed munificence itself to her. And so it
came to pass that at last the search for work
came to an end.

The days and weeks passed slowly, and to
one at least of the women who lived in that
cottage on the outskirts of the great town
they were full of weariness. It is not easy
to lay down one's life; courage fails at
times, and it almost seems to us as if, in
spite of ourselves, that we shall rise up and
take it again.

And just about this time Mary began to
watch Maggie attentively when she was sure
the eyes of the worker would not be raised;
scrutinizing her as she stood at the open door,
or when passing in front of one of the
windows. And after one of these close
scrutinies Mary's face would become troubled
and thoughtful, and she would be silent for

a long time, and would leave it to Maggie
to begin the conversation—not that this was
done by design on Mary's part.

One night when Mary had been lying
awake for some hours, she turned upon her
pillow, and, after assuring herself by listening
to the way her husband breathed that he
was awake, she told him of the thought which
had been troubling her concerning Maggie.
Then the two talked together in low tones,
the woman pityingly and urgently, the man
prosaically, and sometimes even coldly and
harshly; but Mary understood his mood.
How often had she told Maggie that this
strike was making the outside of him rough
and ill-mannered, but his heart was right
enough; she could make sure of her Tom
in that. At length the man said—

"Like enough it's for this she's run away.
And I dare say you're right, my lass, in
saying that we should keep her. If our
little Annie were to have such a slip when
she comes to be a big grown girl—which God

forbid !—I should hope somebody would give her shelter."

And so it came to pass that Maggie took up her fixed abode with Tom and Mary Kesteven.

BOOK VII.

CHAPTER I.

LINKS.

WHEN Maggie's letter, which she had left reared up against the little speckled looking-glass in her bedroom, was found and read the morning after she left her home, mingled feelings of pain and anger rose in the hearts of father and mother. Why had she done such a thing, they asked, amid tears and reproaches, when they had always been so kind to her? What could have tempted her to leave a home where for many years to come, there would be plenty? Ay, and if Matthew did not wed—and surely it seemed likely enough now

that he would not, for when had Matthew
Tindale been known to think more of one
girl than another—would there not always
be his fireside to sit by? But, putting away
all this, if she really wished, as she said in her
letter, to be making something for herself, why
had she not told them? It would have been
time enough to run away when they had refused
her request. And so the two old people sat
in the early morning, weeping and bemoaning
the unkindness of their child.

Meanwhile Matthew paid little heed to
them, sitting in a fit of nervous abstraction,
the keen watchfulness of his glance, and the
habit that he had acquired of late, of turning
his head to one side, as though listening for
some sound, more painfully apparent. Then,
when he began to hear the questions which
were being raised by the two old people, he set
his teeth, and the expression of his eyes became
hard and firm. Why had Maggie done this?
He knew, or, at least, so he told himself—she
wanted to get away from Staneby before the

story of her shame was known. And bitter hatred against the man whom he had hurled over the cliffs rose in his heart.

He sat before the breakfast table, where the food stood untasted, hatred raging within him as it raged that night, when he set out to try to force on the marriage, which, in his rustic ignorance, he believed would undo the moral injury of seduction.

Would that the man were alive that he might strike him dead again ! And with this thought in his mind, Matthew sprang to his feet, bringing his clenched fist down upon the table with a force that shook the crockery ; while upon his lips and half spoken, was a tremendous oath, which, however, he checked, for the recollection of Maggie and her secret came to him. What was he doing ? Was he going to betray her ? He lifted his hand from the table, and passed it, as if in confusion of thought, over his eyes. Then it slipped nervelessly down, and he looked in his mother's face, the flush of anger suddenly fading, while an expression of fear came, which slowly deepened into one of dread, as the tension of his jaws relaxed, and his face turned to an ashen whiteness.

For a minute silence fell upon the occupants of the kitchen. Then Mrs. Tindale said in a high trembling voice—

" Never set ye lips to swear at her."

" I didn't swear at her, mother—I mean, I will not swear at her again."

Matthew shivered. It was only another prevarication, only another of those lesser lies, of which his life seemed full. He turned his face from his mother, and looked out of the window. Of late he had come to look very often across the wide stretch of country. An undefined emotion, half hope, half aspiration, seemed to come to him with soothing power, whenever his eyes rested, where, bounded by no mountain, the grey horizon line was lost in indefinite haze which might have been land or sea or sky. In that far distance there lay a stillness—a deep and vast forgetfulness to him

" My lad, ye'll hev to go an' seek her."

It was Mrs. Tindale who spoke, and again Matthew turned and looked in his mother's face. He did not answer her at once, multitudinous thoughts chasing each other through his mind. Was it to be his task to bring back Maggie, when she was trying to hide herself? To bring her back when she was endeavouring to save her parents from the trouble which would come with a knowledge of her shame? Would he be justified in seeking for her, knowing, as he believed he did, the reason which had sent her a fugitive from her home? Matthew's thoughts never went beyond the one reason, and he did not connect her flight in any way with himself: the strength of the sister's love went beyond the ken of the brother.

" I tell ye, my lad, ye must go after her, an' bring her back."

Still Matthew did not speak. But something in the expression of his mother's face changed the current of his thoughts, and

Maggie came into his mind as in distress, homeless, and without a guardian. For fully half a minute he was silent, but when at last he spoke it was with more composure than he had hitherto shown. " We're talking of our Maggie as if she was after something shameful ! " he said. " Leave her alone for a bit, mother—and leave me alone."

" Ye might hev been let into this plan o' hers—an' more shame to ye if ye hev—from the way ye talk." Here Mrs. Tindale ceased weeping, and, drying her eyes on her apron, looked angrily at her son.

" I know nothing of her plans. But I fancy somehow "—Matthew hesitated, fearful of saying too much—" that she has been tired o' Staneby for a bit."

" An' what should make her tired o' Staneby, I should like to know ? "

" I don't know. People do get tired of a place sometimes."

" See nonsense ! Why, I'd never be tired of any place so long as I had yer father, an'

you, an' Maggie. It isn't *places* that one
wants, it's *people*."

"I cannot tell ye." And Matthew shook
his head, as if the reiteration of the question
wearied him.

"It's just contrariness with her, that's what
it is. She always held up her head as if
no one was fit to speak to, an' now she
goes an' says they're not fit for her to live
with."

Matthew ventured to remark there was
nothing said about that in the letter.

"Well, I know there isn't; but it's all the
same; she means it if she doesn't say it," returned Mrs. Tindale irritably, smoothing her
apron with sharp strokes over her knees.

"Come, mother, ye're put out." It was the
old man who spoke.

"An' who wouldn't be put out with such
gander-flanking? To think of her goin' off all
by herself, an' nobody knows where. I hevn't
a bit o' patience with her."

"Oh, mother, have patience with her; there's

a deal o' things in this world that not even them 'at 's dearest knows anything on."

Matthew could not help pleading thus far; more he dared not say, for to plead for his sister as he could plead would be to betray her.

" I can't hev any patience, I tell ye, puttin' yer father an' me about like this. An' think what kind of a cock-fightin' story I'll hev to make up to excuse her! For I can tell ye I won't hev t' neighbours know that she's gone off like this."

" Say what she says herself, that she's gone to seek a situation—— "

" Yes," interrupted Mrs. Tindale, " an' a bonnie tale they'll think it when they see you an' me set off too; all of us wantin' situations, just as if we were boys an' girls loosed from school."

" Mother, it isn't like you to talk o' this way." And Matthew gave a sigh of utter weariness.

Mrs. Tindale burst into tears. Her son had spoken truly; it was not like her to show so much irritation ; but the excitement and annoyance had been more than she could bear with equanimity, and after the fashion of some women she had goaded herself into a fit of temper, lest in the end she should give way to tears.

" I isn't really cross at her, bless her heart, an' that ye might know as well as me, Mattha. But I've been fairly put out, an' so I've just rived away at things a bit with my tongue. It eases one's heart sometimes, Mattha, to do't. A good fit o' scoldin' 'll bring a lot of ease, an' stop one hevin' a weight here just for all the world like a bit o' lead." And the speaker laid her hand on her chest.

" Does it, mother ? " And Matthew gave another deep sigh of weariness. He was wondering if a storm of words would lift the weight which laid on him.

The thought changed the flickering play of emotion, and his attention was diverted from the stream of words which again flowed from his mother's lips, and he began pacing the kitchen backward and forward excitedly. He seemed to be listening for some sound, and to be looking about him for the sight of something which never came.

"My lad, you and I must go and look for her. Poor lassie, it'll never do to leave her to hersel."

"Yes, mother, we will go and look." But the speaker still strode on, never glancing even for a moment at his mother.

"My lad, we must go now. I'll away an' get my shawl."

"Not now, mother; not now." And the speaker strode about more restlessly. The sounds for which he had been listening were falling on his ears : for seeming is reality, and reality is seeming. To Matthew nothing could be more real than those ever-haunting sounds, and his attention turned itself wholly upon them.

"Ye can't go to seek her to-day," put in the old man. "Wait until she writes and says where she is. Mebbe we'll hev a letter to-morrow, and then ye can go straight to her. If ye go now ye'll mebbe hev to seek through England, Scotland, an' Ireland afore ye find her."

Of what use was it to go to look for Maggie without a single clue as to the direction which she had taken? The old man spoke truly. And this Mrs. Tindale must have thought, for she dropped silently into a chair.

Meanwhile Matthew strode up and down the kitchen, and round and round, his eyes never so much as falling in a passing glance upon either of his parents. He had forgotten them; he had forgotten Maggie; he had forgotten everything but the part which he himself had played in the tragedy. The remembrance of it was crushing him. He must go to work in the smithy—that was the only thing which could bring relief. He must go and swing the heaviest hammer he could find. He must go and get thick bars of iron, heating them till they were turned to the fierce white light of the sun, that their heat might be to him as the heat and burning of his remorse, and their whiteness as the fierce agony of despair which consumed him; and then he must lay them across the anvil, and scourge and beat and smite, until the wild clashing mingled with the clash and din which rose within his soul.

Mechanically his hand sought for the fastening of the door, and as it felt for it a figure, which had been crouching outside, started up and, with a swift movement, made its way round to the end of the house. It was the figure of a man, small, mean, despicable, and wearing rusty black clothes, and having a roll of black calico twisted about its waist.

But Matthew had no eyes for it as he stepped across the threshold with his head held up, though with that stooping forward of the neck and shoulders which had been common with him of late.

A wisp of straw was soon thrust amongst the dead cinders; the handle of the bellows

was moved slowly up and down ; the coal
caught and kindled with crimson edges, until
there was an up-leaping column of flame and
beneath it a glow of white heat. Then
Matthew prepared for work, rolling up his
shirt-sleeves, and taking off his collar and tie.
But something made him pause and throw
aside the leathern apron before it could be
fastened on. An exciting and a feverish
thought must have taken hold of him, judging
by the expression of his face, and the deep
flush that spread even to his neck. Yes, he
would have another look, to make sure that it
was safe ! He did not feel as if he could begin
his work until he had done that. He had
looked at it yesterday, and the day before,
indeed on what day had he not looked ? To
peer into that great chest at the further side
of the smithy, and to lift from it the collection
of old iron, horse-shoes, coulters, harrow-teeth
—a hateful kind of work, and yet, though he
was repelled by it, a task that ever fascinated
and enthralled him. He felt always as if he

could have spent the whole day in gazing at what that chest contained, when the iron had been lifted from it; he ever wanted to assure himself that what lay beneath was perfectly safe, though the sight of it made his blood stagnate, and his eyeballs burn into his brain.

It was only a white kitle, a linen jacket, with the ,pocket torn down at one side, and the sleeves frayed and chafed. What could there be in this to move him ?

Matthew raised the heavy oak lid, and took the iron bit by bit out of the chest, until at length the linen jacket lay exposed. This done he stood looking down at it, with a satisfaction which was at the same time mingled with a shrinking horror. He would like to lift it up and examine it. He had never touched it since that night when he had torn it off and hidden it in the chest. He wondered if he could touch it. He wondered whether he would have strength to lift it up. He was longing to see if the pocket were torn down as deeply as he thought. He even began to speculate, in the case of any one else seeing it, upon the possibility of the tearing of the pocket betraying him. He had never thought about that before. Yes, he must look at it just to see whether other eyes besides his own could see the fingers of a dead man's hand tightly locked upon the linen, and whether other ears could hear the sound which the rent had made. So thinking, he stooped, and with cold clammy fingers caught hold of the kitle and lifted it from the chest.

Meanwhile the man who skulked round the end of the house had come from his hiding-place, and was watching Matthew's movements through a crack in the shutters that still closed the smithy window. To see the blacksmith light the fire and prepare himself for work was of little interest, and scarcely worth the risk of discovery; but when Matthew's demeanour so suddenly and curiously changed, and when the lid of the oak chest was raised, the man who watched smiled as he gnawed his blackened thumb-nail, thinking meanwhile to himself that his many hours of watching were at length going to be repaid.

Piece by piece the iron was lifted out and laid on the floor; a coulter, a clanking chain, a handful of rusty horse-shoes, then another coulter, and here Matthew shifted his position, and the watcher could no longer see each object as it was removed. The thumb-nail was gnawed angrily, and the loose, unshapely lips of the man were opened to allow for the muttering of an oath. But he was not going to be baulked in so easy a way, just when it was likely there was something to be seen which Matthew Tindale would wish to keep from view. Perhaps even yet there might be something hidden in the chest which would be a tangible witness of guilt. How he longed to bring Sidney Aschenburg's death home to Matthew Tindale. He was certain now in his own mind that the young Squire had been hurled over the cliffs by the blacksmith, but he could never find anything which could be brought up as evidence, although he had been watching and waiting patiently. He himself had seen Matthew in the Derthwaite woods on the night when Sidney Aschenburg met his death, with bruised face and cut lip, and jacket torn and disarranged ; therefore he could give evidence which would strongly buttress up an accusation made by another, but he knew his own character to be such that none would listen to him were he alone to turn accuser.

And so he crept softly round the smithy to the open door, and stood there, with his eyes held just past the lintel. But when he saw Matthew, after a long pause in which nothing had been taken out of the chest, lift up something slowly and hesitatingly, which he held at arm's length, the mean figure of the watcher came wholly into view, all precautions forgotten in the diabolical joy which seized him. For a few brief seconds he stood and looked at the square-shouldered figure of the man, who, with his back turned upon the door, was unconscious of any intruder, hatred and malignant ecstasy written upon his face.

Then Matthew dropped the linen jacket, and turned round.

In a moment the shoemaker—for it was he—seemed as if about to obey an impulse which prompted flight. He swung hurriedly on his heels, catching hold of the doorpost so as to accelerate his movement; then almost as swiftly did he twist himself back again, his craven-heartedness showing itself in his face, mingled with an expression of bravado. He shrank and cowered in the presence of the man whom he longed to see done to death; and yet, because it was an opportunity for torture such as he had never yet had, he was determined that his feelings should not drive him from the field.

The blacksmith stood and faced him with a set, rigid expression. Without tangible thought, there was no place for wonder in his mind concerning the length of time the shoemaker might have been standing on the threshold, no place for doubt whether the contents of the chest might or might not have been seen. But in a moment a fit of half-frenzied anger took possession of him, and, without any warning, he leaped suddenly forward, his arms falling with the weight of some huge beast of prey upon the shoulders of the man who was spying upon his actions from within the shelter of the smithy doorway.

"You d—d liar! You scoundrel! There——" And the spare figure of the shoemaker was flung across the road.

There was no struggle; only the lifting up, as it were, by Titanic hands, of some loathsome reptile, and the abhorrent casting of it aside.

The door of the smithy closed, and the next moment a fierce blast roared up the chimney, and flame and sparks rose high above the low roof into the air. Then this ceased, and mighty blows, swift, fierce, and strong, rang out upon the anvil, mingled with the voice of a man singing the refrain of a drinking-song, which was repeated again, and again, and yet again.

CHAPTER II.

THE LAST NIGHT AT THE GAROD ARMS.

THE physical soreness from which Neddy Kendal suffered all day in consequence of the rough method by which he had been ejected from the smithy, was as nothing compared with the soreness under which his spirit laboured. He had of late wrought himself into the belief that the blacksmith was being drawn firmly beneath his clutches, and that he was passing from a state of impassive ignorance into one of full consciousness, that not only did he, Kendal, suspect him of having been instrumental in Sidney Aschenburg's death, but that he was actually in possession of facts which would form strong links of circumstantial evidence against him. His anger and humiliation were great, therefore, when this very man whom he had taught himself to regard as his trembling victim, had, with an assumption of righteous scorn, turned upon him and hurled him off his path with as little ado as a gardener would a worm.

To Neddy, it seemed as if such scorn could only have its basis in a conscience free from crime ; and he began with wrath to wonder if, after all, he had been mistaken in supposing that because he had seen Matthew with swollen and cut lip, and with a rent in his linen jacket on the very night of Mr. Sidney Aschenburg's disappearance, he was necessarily instrumental to it.   And again, might it not have been a mere accident that Matthew had shown signs of being troubled and disturbed that night at the Garod Arms, when the talk had been turned upon the verdict given at the coroner's inquest, Neddy himself—the wish being father to the thought in his malicious heart—saying, how for his part he thought it should have been "murder"? But how was it that the shoemaker had been allowed to use the subject of Sidney Aschenburg's disappearance as a kind of poisoned dart upon the blacksmith, plying him with a word now and again that would cause a steely look to come into his eyes, and an expression of hardness to his lips? If he were innocent of the crime which was ever covertly hinted at, surely such hints would have been resented. Then, again, why, unlike everybody else who could remain in Staneby to look at the young Squire's funeral procession, had he gone up to the moor and walked about there like a man who was off his head? Certainly it seemed as if he were trying to be as far as possible from that which lay beneath the coffin-lid.

Neddy sat before his cobbler's table, feelings of venomous anger in his heart. It mattered very little to him that he had been caught in the act of playing the spy, and had suffered ignominious treatment, of which his limbs and back ached in continual reminder; but to have to face the thought that possibly, after all, Matthew was not guilty of the crime which he longed to bring home to him, was to be vexed and tried in a way he could not bear.

As hour after hour went by, he began to pluck up a little courage, and told himself that things might not be so bad as they seemed. He must watch more narrowly the expression of Matthew's face when others spoke to him. He, himself, must grow accustomed to meet the blacksmith's eye without flinching. He must train his ear to learn the meaning of every tone of Matthew's voice. He would do it, he told himself, he would do it yet; he would live to see Matthew Tindale swing for a crime. And the thumb-nail was gnawed down to the quick.

So that night when he stepped into the kitchen at the Garod Arms, his eyes at once went furtively round to see if the blacksmith were there, and not as usual to note if a chair remained unoccupied in the warmest and most comfortable' corner for him to take.

No one moved with the kind of hospitable gesture which seems to say, " you are welcome." Only Tom Farrar said, " Well, Neddy." But this he was in duty bound to do from his position as host, at least so Tom himself would have said.

But the shoemaker was accustomed to this kind of thing, and paid little heed to it. It was of greater importance to him to find that Matthew was seated there, and that a vacant chair stood opposite to him. So he moved across the kitchen, while, in the pause that followed the landlord's brief welcome, the grit of the sanded floor could be heard beneath his trailing feet.

" Yer soles are fond o' this earth, Neddy ; they don't lift theirsels clean up as if they'd like to be away."

Neddy had been looking at the back of the blacksmith's head from under his eyebrows, but he turned at this, and scowled at the face of the speaker.

"Who meddles wi' my soles, I'd like to know?" he snarled.

"Not the parson, I guess; they'd be too black for him," answered the same man, with a laugh, as he nudged the arm of his neighbour.

"Every man's house is his castle, and every man owns t' boots 'at belongs to him, an' so, gentlemen, if ye please we'll hev a pleasanter subject for conversahin." It was of course Tom Farrar who said this.

"Couldn't hev a pleasanter for Neddy. He likes well to talk of hissel," remarked the rosy-faced butcher; and a peal of laughter followed his remark, for rustics, when bent on amusement, laugh very readily. .

"I'll give ye all summat that'll make ye laugh at t' other side o' yer faces;" said Neddy fiercely, clasping with both hands the seat of the Windsor chair on which he had seated himself, and holding himself, as it were, tightly

down ; not that he was afraid of springing
involuntarily on his tormenters, but the tight
clasp and downward pressure on the chair
gave him an artificial sense of strength.

"That's it, Neddy ;" and Mrs. Farrar
stretched her bony hand over his shoulder as
she placed a glass of beer on a table in front
of him. " Set to work, an' let's see how ye'll
manage it. I guess I'd begin with Mattha—
the laugh's allas at t' wrong side o' *his* face."

Matthew, unlike most of the men, had taken
off his hat and hung it on one of the pegs near
the door when he came in, and was now sitting
with the light from the hanging lamp falling
full upon him. He had aged very much within the last two months. The fair hair was of
a lighter shade upon the temples, and any one
looking closely could see that this was because
much of it was faded and grey. Minute zig-
zag lines were spread round the eyes as a net-
work ; the eyes themselves were sunken, and
when they were not lighted by nervous
feverishness, were dull and looked out with a

gaze that seemed to long for the sleep which may stretch into thousands of years, or into an eternity of years—for who can tell ? Patient endurance sat upon the lips and brow, but with it there was a worn expression, and a tired leaning of the head ; and lassitude was shown in the frame and limbs, a back-ground of lassitude as it were to every action, such as comes with a tenacious and insidiously growing disease.

When Mrs. Farrar spoke, Matthew turned his eyes from the shoemaker to her, but without any change of expression coming into his face. He seemed to be watching and listening abstractedly. He had not laughed when all the other men had broken into their fit of merriment, had only looked from one to the other until his gaze finally settled upon Neddy.

In spite of the shoemaker's determination to watch him closely, all this had been unobserved by him, so greatly had he been vexed by the laughter and clumsy jests. When, however,

Mrs. Farrar spoke, Neddy was brought back to a recollection of the task he had assigned himself, and he instantly fixed his small close-set eyes upon Matthew's, which, with their sad tired expression, were lifted to Mrs. Farrar.

The landlady's words would yield him a subject with which to begin upon, was Neddy's thought. And so, still holding firmly by his chair, for since the episode of the morning Neddy quailed more than was his wont in attacking Matthew, he said—

" Ye've likely always pleasant thoughts, that ye keep see a smile on yer face."

The words fell upon Matthew in a dim kind of way ; but he made no sign of having heard them.

" I've noticed ye've always hed a laugh or a smile for everybody since t' night t' young squire was drowned, just as if ye were right well pleased with yersel." The shoemaker took a tighter grip of his chair ; for with these words Matthew had slowly moved his head and looked at him.

It was a quarter of a minute before the blacksmith gave signs of having taken in the meaning of the words. Then his demeanour suddenly changed; the lassitude left him ; his broad chest was straightened and his head held up ; his lips parted and he laughed. But the sound of the laugh was devoid of all that makes laughter ; it was no laugh at all, and Matthew himself must have felt it, for he tried again, opening his mouth wider and sending out louder and shriller tones.

"It's a queer thing to laugh at, any way ; " and this time the shoemaker spoke the sentiments of the company. "I used to think you and young Aschenburg were grand sort o' friends, but ye never seemed to take on about his death as I should ha' thought ye'd ha' done."

"Didn't I ?" Matthew's eyes had brightened and the firm look of enduring patience was gone. He now sat forward on his chair, his head held eagerly, his eyes looking first at the row of men on his right, and then turning to

look at the row on his left. Quite abruptly
he checked himself in this, and throwing himself back in his chair, beckoned to Mrs. Farrar,
and when she came up to him, told her he
wanted a pint of beer with sixpenny worth of
rum in it.

The men sitting near enough to hear
Matthew's order paused a moment, some in
their talking, some in their smoking. They
had never before known Matthew drink anything beyond a glass of simple beer.

"An' why do ye think young Mr. Aschenburg an' me should be friends?" asked
Matthew, when he had turned back to the
shoemaker, experiencing a new and strange
delight in the danger which lurked for him
in the handling of such a theme.

"Oh, I don't know that I do now. It was
my mistake, I tell ye. I guess ye wanted him
off t' face o' t' earth."

Matthew had lifted the glass of rum and
beer from Mrs. Farrar's tray, and was raising
it slowly to his lips, his eyes fixed on the

shoemaker's face; but when the last words
fell from Neddy, he paused, then, stretching
out his hand with the glass in it at arm's
length, looked fixedly at its contents. There
was something in the action, coupled with
the expression that came like a blast of
passion into his face, which arrested the
attention of the men who had for the most
part been talking in groups, heedless of what
was passing between Matthew and the shoemaker, and they broke off suddenly to watch
him.

" He's drunk ! " exclaimed the butcher under
his breath, but not in a low enough tone to
escape Matthew's ear.

" No, I'm not." Matthew spoke with his
eyes still fixed upon the glass. " I'm not
drunk, and, by God, I'm not going to be,
either." And before the last words escaped
his lips, he hurled the glass with it's contents
to the further end of the kitchen.

There was a momentary silence, and then a
subdued murmur of surprised exclamations,

interspersed with not a few rustic oaths; while
above it all, and as the tones of a shrill
trumpet to which other instruments are but
an accompaniment, rang Mrs. Farrar's voice,
scolding, upbraiding, questioning, and giving
screams of defiance.

"I'd like to see ye do 't again, that's all,"
she said, as she leaned between the two men
in order to shake her fist within sight of
Matthew's eyes.

"Whisht," thundered Tom Farrar's voice.

"Yes, you do 't again, an' I'll let ye see!"

Matthew swept down the woman's threaten-
ing hand without so much as glancing at it,
and then, folding his arms across his chest,
looked, with a face that was whitening round
the nostrils and mouth, straight into the eyes
of the shoemaker.

"Now then, Neddy, I'll stand an ounce o'
tobacco it was your fault." Bill Taylor's
voice came with an expostulating tone from
the far end of the kitchen, and those who
looked could see how he was drawing up his

long legs with the evident intention of rising from his seat.

"Keep yer meddlesome sel' to yer sel', if ye please," returned the shoemaker with a "yow" of splenetic anger. "Mattha an' me can settle our business our two sels." And Neddy turned his narrow, fox-like face upon his victim.

"Well, an' what is 't we've got to settle?" The pallor was creeping up to Matthew's temples. But he sat erect, and his face wore a look of composure and endurance.

"I should think ye can guess pretty well what I mean." The shoemaker hugged himself more closely to his chair, and forced a smile to his lips. "Ye needn't tell me ye don't know. You an' me could settle a bonnie thing atween us."

"We could settle many things atween us— many things that hev happened within t' last few months. Do ye think, Neddy Kendal, that I hevn't seen how yer eyes hev been turned on me at all times, an' that yer feet hev followed me pretty nigh wherever I went? There's a big score, I tell ye, atween us, an' I'll settle it any time ye've a mind." The speaker's hands clenched with an involuntary movement, and for a second he seemed as if about to spring up from his chair.

"Perhaps ye'd like to settle 't as ye settled another score — oh no, I'se not goin' to say anything about it; I'se not goin' to peach on what I saw."

"I'll settle 't now with ye. Come on."

This time Matthew did spring to his feet, and tearing coat and waistcoat off, began to roll up his shirt sleeves, while the deathly pallor swept over his neck and ears.

"Now then, now then! Come, gentlemen, if you please———" And Tom Farrar hastily pushed back his chair, and stepped up to the small round table which yet remained as a protection in front of the shoemaker.

"Don't ye touch him wi' t' end o' yer finger." It was Bill Taylor who spoke, placing himself immediately in front of Matthew, and

trying to lay restraining hands on the blacksmith. "Who cares what Neddy Kendal
does?" he continued, "he's the illest cur
in the village. I'd think no more o' anything he said an' did to me, than I'd think
o' the bite of a rat or a weasel, or any such
like varment."

"But ye don't know, ye don't understand.
Get by, I say."

"I'll not get by. To-morrow ye'd be sorry
ever ye'd laid hands on such a chap."

"Get by." And this time the blacksmith
took hold of the loosely built figure of the man
before him, and pushed him aside.

"I'll not touch him. Ye needn't be afraid,"
continued Matthew, in a loud excited tone,
looking round at the men present, who for the
most part had risen from their seats. "I
thought at first that I would take him up an'
shake the life out of his body. But I won't
do it—I won't do that. I've had enough on't,
I tell ye. Ye don't understand my meaning,
but it's no matter. I tell ye I'll not touch

him ; I've had enough on't." The speaker's excitement increased, and he stood with hands laid upon his hips, his chest heaving and his face distorted.

" Ay, Mattha, a quarrel with such as him isn't worth a thought. I'd put it away out o' yer mind." And again Bill Taylor placed himself in front of the blacksmith.

" Stand by, I say." With these words Matthew put out one of his arms, and with a strength born of passion, swept Bill Taylor aside with as little ado as if he had been a child. " One o' ye said just now I was drunk. What wad ye think if I tell ye I've been drunk for months—ay, for months ? "

The butcher catching Tom Farrar's eye at this moment, tapped his forehead significantly.

" Eh, ye think I'm mad as well ? An' ye're right, more right than ye've ever guessed. I've been both mad and drunk. I've been driven —driven—driven. I've seen such things as none of you hev ever seen, an' I've heard such things as none of you hev ever heard. An'

Neddy Kendal hes watched me. He's looked at me, an' he's harried me. Sometimes I think it's Neddy that hes done it all."

"Ye liar, ye! Don't ye go an' say *I* put him into t' water." And the shoemaker, cowering and pale, loosened his hold of the chair and shook his fist at the speaker.

"It's you that has driven me into feeling that if I'se silent any longer I shall go mad," continued Matthew, taking no notice of the interruption. "It's you that has hunted me down. It's you that made me feel that I must turn, an' hev no more on't. Ye didn't think it, Neddy, but you were doing your best to made me an honest man. An' ye've made me one, for, by God, I'll hev no more on't. I'll not go any longer sneaking about pretending to be what I isn't. I'll tell to-night—ay, before you, Neddy Kendal—I'll tell to-night what's been hidden in my breast all these months."

" Well, speak t' truth, then, an' let's hev no putting on to other folks."

The shoemaker's eyes flashed with malicious joy, and he sat on his hands and rocked himself with a sort of fiendish glee backward and forward.

"Now then, mates, I want ye to look at me straight in the face, every one." Matthew paused and caught with the back of his hand some of the drops of sweat that trickled down his temples. Then he continued, but speaking with great effort, "Ye'll all remember that night when—when—— How is it likely ye'll remember? . . . It was a moonlight night, I tell ye—bright moonlight, such as makes everything look as fair as daylight. I'd been working up at Seatenner better part o' the day. An' I mind how I came by the moor, an' how I saw Bella Hind. She was bringing home t' cows, an' I helped her to drive them."

Matthew raised his eyes from the group of men who had gathered round him. There was an expression in them of intense suffering, and the last sentence was spoken abstractedly, as though he talked to himself.

"Aye we had begun to think you an' Bella would make a match of it," said a voice from the fireplace. And then several others joined assentingly.

"Bella Hind an' me? Bella Hind!" The eyes of the speaker came slowly down upon the circle of faces. "Not Bella Hind. She an' me can never wed."

Unutterable anguish rang in the tone with which these words were said, and the men, rough, ignorant rustics though they were, drew closer together and closer to Matthew, as if they would show their pity for a trouble which they could not comprehend. All but Neddy Kendal; he still rocked and swung himself with enjoyment of the scene.

"Yes, I came home from the moor," Matthew went on slowly, passing one hand over his forehead as though his mind were too disturbed for him to trace the course of events clearly. "I came home, and then . . . No, I cannot mind of the next thing I did. I cannot tell whether I went to work in t' smithy or not."

"Well, don't fash yourself about that, old chap. Tell us what it is that's putting ye about; just rough like, an' as it comes into yer mind." And Bill Taylor laid his hand with a clumsy movement of affection upon Matthew's shoulder.

"Yes, I'll go straight at it."

And with the words Matthew's mighty form seemed to tower head and shoulders above the other men, and his face, as if it courted it, came under the light of the hanging lamp. The sentences were toiling up from his chest, and his voice trembled, its tone so thick as almost to render the words unintelligible. And the men craned their necks and made a slight, though perfectly noiseless, movement toward him.

"I met him in the wood just above the Devil's Pot. I tell ye, then I had no thoughts of murdering him."

"But who, Mattha—who did ye meet?" The butcher's rosy face was paling, and his eyes showed horror and perplexity.

" Whisht !" called out Tom Farrar.

" I met—why I met *him*. I met Mr. Sidney
Aschenburg on the fisherman's path. He was
standing there with the moonlight shining
upon him. An' I tell ye I was mad with
anger, an' I hedn't rightly made up my mind
what I was going to say to him, for I didn't
think I should see him till I got to Derth'aite.
An' so I said something to him—I can't
remember a word of it now. But I called to
him to fight. An' then because he hed a little
stick of his hand, I pulled it away from him
an' threw it right back into t' wood. But we
didn't strip off our coats—somehow there
didn't seem any time—but we just fell to
and fought."

" But what hed ye quarrelled about ?"
This time it was Tom Farrar who interrupted,
and the butcher who resented the interruption.

" No, I'll never tell what we quarrelled
about. That's my secret. Only me and him
knows." Again Matthew paused, and again

his hand went to his forehead, as if he had a difficulty in framing his sentences connectedly. " We fought on a bit o' ground there, that's clear of bushes an' ferns. There's nothing on it but short grass. I don't know how we got on, an' whether he hit me or whether I hit him. Somehow nothing of the beginning of it is clear to me. I can only remember rightly about the time when I got him to the ground. I mind now of the rage that came into me "—the speaker shuddered and drew back as if from some intense physical agony—" an' I made up my mind then that I would hev his life. From that time I can tell ye everything I did. I caught hold of one of his arms and clapped it down to his side, holding it there while I tried to get hold of the other. An' he twisted an' turned about in front o' me, until at last his foot slipped an' he flung out his free arm to save himself, when I caught it. Then I forced him inch by inch nearer the river. He hed his back to it ; I'd mine to the wood. My boots had a better hold o' the grass than his ; an' his slipped and slided an' always gave way with him, little bit by little bit. At last he got on the rock, and so having the best hold, he gave a great struggle and broke away from me. Then he struck right for my face ; but I caught hold again of him, an' this time of his wrists, so that he could no longer help himself. An' then we twisted an' pushed, an' he cried out if I meant to put him over."

A spell of horror had fallen upon the group of listening men, and they watched with bated breath the face and gestures of the man, who no longer recited his story under powerful self-restraint, but emotionally, and in a way that threatened complete loss of control.

"He gave one last struggle an' got one of his han's free. Then he laid hold of my kitle, an' atween us we tore it, him pulling one way an' me another. It was after this that I lifted his feet over the rock "—the speaker caught his hand down over his eyes and held it there for a moment—" but they always came

back again and tried to twist theirselves round
mine. I can feel them now, and I can hear
their scrape, scrape against the edge of the
rock ! Oh, God . . . I pushed him back
again, till his han's began to cling to mine,
an' would not let them go. Then I thought
I was never going to get him into t' river. . . .
But he went quite suddenly, an' as he slipped
away from me he cried out. . . . I hear his
voice day an' night, day an' night. I feel
his han's taking hold o' my han's, an' sometimes I try to put them away, and sometimes
I try to hold them fast that he mayn't go
over t' edge o' t' rock. But he always goes,
always goes, though his han's are holding
mine, an' his feet are about my ankles. He
is always falling, falling, an' I am always
holding, holding."

Matthew paused, his chest working with
convulsive heaves. He was pallid, and his
hair was damp with the sweat of his agony ;
and his eyes were sunken and deep lines
had come round his mouth. . Vacantly he

looked round at the group of men, some of whom seemed stupefied, while others were horror-struck; and then, finding no one spoke, he said in a questioning tone, as though he wondered at their silence—

"Neddy saw me coming back. He was hiding behind a wall—— "

"Ye liar! I wasn't hiding," yelled the shoemaker.

"Neddy was beside a wall in the quarry wood, an' he saw me with my torn kitle an' my bruised face."

The eyes of the men were instantly turned from Matthew to Neddy, and, like the breaking of the waters of a sullen sea, they uttered questions in low tones, hurried and fragmentary.

"Yes, I saw him. An' his kitle was torn, an' his face looked as if he had been fightin'. Oh yes; ye may depend upon 't, it's true enough what he says."

"An' what hed ye to do wi' 't?" Bill Taylor's hulking frame towered threateningly over the shoemaker, and he looked fiercely at the upturned, narrow face.

"I'd nothing to do wi' 't. I'se a witness, that's all."

"It's a deal liker that you put t' young squire into t' river than Mattha. Every chap about t' place knows that you used to go after his hares."

"Now then!" And here Neddy Kendal screamed out his words, and flung one hand gesticulatingly toward Matthew. "He's told you hissel how he did it. Don't ye go turnin' it on to me."

"My lads, I did it." For the first time that night Matthew's voice rang clearly and steadily, and it was heard above the babel.

"Yes, he did it. Mind that!"

"Neddy had no hand in't. Remember, all o' ye, that I've said this when the time comes."

Once more the weary eyes were turned from face to face, but the carriage of the head and the proud bearing of the shoulders were of the

Matthew of old.   And then, without a word,
he made for the peg on which his hat hung,
and, lifting it down, went toward the door.

The men watched him as if spell-bound,
none of them bidding him " Good night," or
endeavouring by word or act to detain him.

CHAPTER III.

I HAVE SINNED.

OUT on the road beneath the starlight Matthew lifted up his head. He breathed more freely, even with the full remembrance of that weight of sin upon his soul. There was to be no more duplicity, no more lying, no more shifting of his eyes from honest men. They would all know him now—know him as Matthew Tindale the murderer. From henceforth they would keep apart from him, and he must keep apart from them. But for how long ? Yes, for how long would he be free to go in and out as he chose ? And then he wondered if he would start, as he used to fancy he would, at the sound of the footsteps that, sooner or

later, must inevitably come ; and whether the
tone of the voice that claimed him would jar
upon his ear ; and if his hands would shrink
from the cold clasp of that which would be
slipped round them.

A chill breeze blew fitfully up the valley.
It rustled the leaves upon ivy-covered walls,
and made the twigs of the honeysuckle and
sweet briar growing over cottage doorways
tremble for a moment before suddenly lapsing
into stillness. The night was not very dark,
and the cottages in Staneby could be seen as
masses of velvety shadow against the sky. A
lighted window, here and there, pierced them.
Matthew saw into one from which the blind
was lifted — saw the ruddy glow of the
firelight as it shone upon a ring of youthful
faces.

He walked on quickly, his eyes, after that
one glance through the uncovered window,
fixed on the veiled landscape that lay beyond
the farthest line of cottages. He did not
want to risk seeing another such vision of

all he had lost. The firelight had made him conscious of a chill that was not merely physical; and the smiles on the faces had shown him the impassable gulf which lay between him and other men.

He longed to meet his doom at once, and began wondering when the messengers would come. Would it be that night, or would the next morning be thought soon enough? And would the whole village be astir with life— people standing in the road, or in the door-ways, or in groups where the best view could be obtained? And would Neddy Kendal lead the way, and, bringing the messengers to the door of the smithy, point him out to them that there could be no mistake?

Matthew halted suddenly and pressed one hand heavily on his chest. His thoughts had gone to the two old people whose pride had ever been in their children, and whose boast it was that such a son and daughter could not be found if the whole Fell-side were searched? How could he bear that they should see him led away in shame. And with a swift revulsion of feeling he shrank from the doom which a minute before he had longed to court, and a wildly passionate desire came upon him to flee and make his escape.

He stood as if rooted to the spot, his head turning from side to side and his eyes straining themselves and scanning the dark outlines of cottage, field, tree, and hill, as if seeking for a way by which he might escape from the upland valley into lands that knew nothing of his guilt.

At that moment the sound of a footstep fell on his ears.

Were the messengers coming? Were they already on his track? And he made the swift uncertain movements of one who sets off in this direction and then in that, but who always checks himself, and who finally pauses and holds himself at bay.

The beat of the falling footsteps became louder, and Matthew could hear that the pedestrian had stepped off the road on to the grass. There was yet time for escape. Thirty yards must at least lie between them, and the darkness would render pursuit difficult. But although Matthew's pulses bounded and leaped, his feet seemed to be weighted with lead, and his limbs to refuse their office. Another minute and it would be too late. Must he go? Must he stay? The sound of the footsteps was getting louder. Again the same convulsive movement first to this side and then to that, and still the same involuntary hesitation. And now it was too late. He could see the figure of a man coming out of the darkness, and as the figure stepped once more off the grass to the road, the man spoke to him.

"I was just hopin' I'd catch up with ye."

"Is it you, Bill?" And Matthew coughed, in order to clear away the strange tone which he heard in his own voice.

"Ay, who else should it be?"

"I thought; but never mind what I thought." Then with a sudden suspicion,

the speaker added, "But perhaps you've
come about it after all ? "

" Of course I've come about it." But Bill
Taylor and Matthew had not the same things
in their mind. " I've come to ask ye what
grudge it was ye owed him ; for as I'm a livin'
man, I'se sure it's been a big 'un, or ye never
wad hev done what ye did."

" I'll never tell."

" For yer own sake ye must, Mattha."

" I tell ye, I willn't tell if I've to die for it."

There seemed no answer to make to this,
and Bill Taylor stood, feeling a little be-
wildered, the thought alone having a clear
hold upon his mind that Matthew's silence
went farther than was required from a cast-off
lover. For Bill Taylor had got it into his
head that pretty Bella Hind had been the
subject of Matthew's quarrel with the young
squire. Rebuffed, he could say no more, however ; and the two men stood face to face
silently in the dimness of the starlight.

After a time Matthew spoke, but slowly

and hesitatingly, for he had but a short range of words at his command.

"I know what ye'd go on to say: him 'at sins first is t' biggest sinner; for when a body has done a wrong thing it catches up first one an' then another, each doin' a worse thing than him who was in front."

"Ay, that's it.   An' if ye hev a grudge see as other folk could see"—here the speaker's thoughts went again to Bella Hind—"it wad make it lighter for ye."

"But hev ye never thought, Bill Taylor, that somebody must stop that handing on of wrong doin'—that somebody must stand in front on it an' say it shall stop here, for I'll do right?"

Bill Taylor did not reply; he was neither a thinker nor philosopher, and the words puzzled him.

"It's o' no good"— and Matthew's voice thrilled with sadness—"ye cannot save me. I've done wrong an' I must abide by it."

"I wad tell if I were ye," returned his

companion, who with the sense of being defeated in spite of himself, could only repeat his former argument, while his eyes instinctively sought among the shadows for the gable of Bella Hind's house.

"Never, I tell ye. There's some folk that I'll serve until I die."

Bill Taylor was no woman hater; but he could not help wondering to himself, while his eyes still sought among the shadows for that gable, whether any woman was worth such devotion.

"Well, if ye willn't tell, I suppose ye willn't," he quietly rejoined. "But it seems to me that a chap like you must hev hed a gay good reason for doin' it."

And so the two men parted, Bill Taylor moving away uneasily and sadly because his mission had failed.

The breeze came up the valley with its fitful gusts, and whistled round the chimney-stacks and under the eaves. The leafless shrubs trembled violently for a few minutes,

and the ivy gave a long sighing rustle, and
then there was stillness and silence. Soon
the breeze came again. How chill it felt,
and how dispassionately the stars shone.
The darkness was the only kindly thing
that night — the darkness which embraced
everything in its arms; the lowly shrubs, the
trees, the houses, even the mighty hills were
all enfolded by it.

Matthew walked restlessly and quickly.
His world was filled with the fierce light of
guilt; no soft shadows lay within it, no darkness blotted out its shapes and forms; no
kindly mantle veiled all things and brought
with it rest and sleep. The dispassionate
stars were there—vast worlds which mocked
his bitterness; and the breeze came ever up
the valley, but not fitfully—rather blowing
steadily, and bringing with it frost and ice
morsels.

The kitchen window at home showed a
brighter light than that which a fire alone could
give. Matthew looked at it, and the patient

expression of suffering came again into his face. He knew what the light meant; he knew that his father or mother, or perhaps both, were sitting there and waiting for him. Beyond this he did not allow his thoughts to go. The same confession which had been made at the Garod Arms must be made to them sooner or later; but how it was to be done, or where, or when, he did not ask himself. An impression rather than a thought, so dim and formless was it, was present with him, that one more night must be left them of ignorance and rest. And so, because through much suffering he was becoming dull and callous, he put his hand on the latch and entered, without so much as a moment's pause.

Mrs. Tindale was standing at the table, a large blue-checked handkerchief spread out upon it, and in this some articles of clothing neatly folded. She looked up as her son entered, holding in her hand the shirt which she had been about to lay beside the other garments.

"I'se makin' ready, ye see," was her remark, spoken in a way which testified to the certainty she felt of her words being understood; and she looked cheerful and smiled. "Yer father's gone to bed. Poor man! he's put out wi' t' day's work. He'll waken up at mornin' an' things will hev a fresh look-out."

Her son answered never a word; but lifting a chair set it close to the table at which she was working, and, seating himself, laid his arms where the kerchief and table were free from stockings and shirts.

"You an' me'll set off early, Mattha, directly after t' post comes in. Indeed, I'm not a bit sure but what there willn't be a letter. I think Maggie is just as likely to write as not, tellin' us where she is, an' settin' everything straight. Maggie was never one to set off by herself. Why, when she was a little 'un she was always wantin' me to go along with her, or you; she was fonder of you, I think, nor anybody."

Matthew took a deep breath and moved uneasily.

" She's just hed a wild fit in her head, that's been it ; it'll be that hes taken her off, ye may depend on't. Girls is queer things, Mattha. Ye see, when they're young an' hevn't their heads weighted — an' there's nothing so good for doin' that as a bit o' trouble—daft kind o' notions come an' catch them up an' whirl them right away just as if they were feathers. Now, men-folk is different. I'se fonder o' men than I is of women ; they're what ye may call more settle-some-like."

" I think ye're fond enough of both, mother." And a wan smile flitted over Matthew's face as he spoke.

" Well, I don't know. Mebbe I is. I think everybody's kind o' full o' goodness. I only hope we'll find everybody as nice an' pleasant in t' next world as they are in this. That's my worst wish for them."

It was not very clear to whom the " them "

referred ; but perhaps Mrs. Tindale was thinking of the warlike preachers she heard in
chapel occasionally, and who appeared to
her to have a very low opinion of their
neighbours.

"I'se puttin' ye in three shirts, Mattha,
for if we make plenty o' provision we're sure
not to need it." And Mrs. Tindale spread
her broad hand out on the top of the pile
of garments and looked inquiringly at her son.

"I'm not sure, mother, that I'll go with
ye." This was said with an effort, and
Matthew cast a vague, restless look round
the kitchen.

"Whatever for ? Yer father can't go, poor
man ; he always gets so puzzled as soon as
ever we get to t' station. I think it's the
screamin' and the flarin' o' them engines that
does it."

"Mother, ye'd better let Maggie be. I wad
rather she never came back."

"What's taken ye now ? Why, I thought
you an' Maggie were such friends as never

hed been!" And Mrs. Tindale stared at her son in vague astonishment.

"I willn't hev her brought back, mother. I tell ye I willn't hev her brought back to be shamed."

"Who talks o' shame, I'd like to know?"

"Better men nor me hev been brought to shame."

Again the restless eyes went round the kitchen, but the face was in shadow and its pallor hidden.

"Cannot ye speak, lad!"

Matthew's powerful frame swayed forward and his head fell upon the pile of clothes, his hands thrown out and clutching at the edge of the table, while great knots showed where the muscles were contracting in his throat.

"Mattha!" and the broad hand was lifted from the shirts and laid upon the fair closely cropped head.

There was a hoarse inarticulate sound, and then a greater effort was made and words came brokenly. "Mother, I've done a bad job for mysel an' for you—I've fallen very low. I've sinned—I've done a mortal sin——" Here he broke away from her, and, springing to his feet, stood a couple of paces distant, a look of agony upon his face such as it had never worn during his confession at the Garod Arms.

"Go on, my lad." And the frame of the burly Cumbrian woman drooped, and her hands fell upon the table where they spread themselves out helplessly. How white she looked and curiously old; and how thin and sharp her voice had become.

"I've nothing much to tell—an' yet, oh, God, it seems a great thing." Matthew's lips and mouth were parched and the words came thickly. "They said, ye'll remember, that he must hev fallen ower—ye know how everybody said it, the coroner and everybody ; but they were aw wrang—he didn't fall over hissel—it was me—me——"

"Who, Mattha? I don't know what ye're talkin' about."

There was a long pause, and then the answer came.

"Mr. Sidney Aschenburg—it was me 'at pushed him ower."

The woman fell forward upon the table as her son had done, and for a minute consciousness left her. Then she came to herself and wondered what it was that had struck her down—whether it was death, or whether that tight clasp round her heart would never slacken till she ceased to breathe. Then she remembered all, and slowly raised herself. She did not weep—her agony was too great for that—but she breathed with audible sobs which 'at times caught the air convulsively. There was a mist before her eyes so that she could not see her son. But gradually this cleared away, and then she smiled—but what a smile it was—and then she held out shaking arms, her whole frame trembling from head to foot, crying, "My lad, come to me!"

With a sob Matthew rushed forward, and

as a child, with his cheek laid against his mother's, wept out his agony.

The kindly arms wound round his great shoulders, and patted and caressed. And one of the hands stole up to his hair and smoothed it, and then, with a touch as soft as though it had been a gentle lady's, played about his ear.

"My hinny, my hinny!" murmured the mother, in a voice that was choked with sobs.

And the strong man crept closer to her.

More tears fell, more tender words were murmured, until slowly, very slowly, Matthew found relief.

Oh, mother-love, wherein lies the secret of thy soothing power? Is it because time cannot change thee, faults cannot alienate thee, and all else being lost, we can yet turn to thee secure of finding a sympathy which in its wealth of loving-kindness is divine?

BOOK VIII.

CHAPTER I.

THE TRIAL.

It was the 10th of February. A grey sky, heavy sleet showers, and a biting north wind made the day cheerless enough. The assize court had been crowded for some hours, and when the judge took his place, standing room was no longer to be obtained; for the case to be opened that morning was, from local causes, of unusual interest, and also from the fact that several eminent members of the bar were engaged upon it.

It was nearly four months since the messengers whose coming Matthew Tindale had so often pictured, had stepped up to him one morning in the smithy, and, showing him a paper, had told him that he was wanted. Nearly three months since he had laid his hammer down for the last time, saying to the messengers that if they would give him time, he would like to change his coat and speak to his mother who was in the house, and to his father, if by chance he had got back from the stroll which a quarter of an hour before he had said he was going to take. And now he stood a prisoner in the dock with the eyes of the closely packed crowd fixed upon him.

There were humane hearts in the crowd who had been attracted to the scene because of their anxiety as to the issue of the trial; and others who had come to watch the proceedings from a calm scientific love of the workings of the law. While some there were who but desired to gratify the love of torture inherent in a base nature; and others who had come with a low form of curiosity, and who found the torpid blood in their veins quickening, and a savage and forgotten life working in them and growing and strengthening with the food offered, until like their ancestors in some far back age they too longed for blood.

Matthew was much thinner; there was a hollow across each cheek as though two fingers had been impressed upon it, and the outlines of the eye-sockets were sharply defined; and though he stood erect and no longer stooped from the shoulders, the wasting was apparent in the muscles of the chest and neck. The greyness of the hair had increased; and a sickly pallor had taken the place of the once ruddy and brown complexion. But the nervous, over-strained expression of the eyes was gone; quiet gravity and sadness lay in them, while strength and self-sufficiency were upon the firmly closed mouth.

Even yet he was a notable looking man. And the judge leaned forward in his seat, a thin forefinger pressed against the clean-

shaven cheek, the lips delicate and thin like
the finger working as if the mind were in
deep thought, while the long-sighted eyes
took note of each feature, every change of
expression, and the general bearing of the
prisoner at the bar. He was accustomed to
read the faces of men as he would read books;
he loved faces as he loved books, and the
face of this prisoner interested him. But
although he was watching him so closely, he
was listening attentively to the man who was
giving evidence.

"I am a shoemaker by trade. I've lived
in Staneby all my life, and have known
Mattha Tindale ever since he was a boy.
I remember t' night of t' 13th of October.
I was in t' Derthwaite quarry wood between
the hours of nine and ten. I heard some one
coming trampling through t' breckins as if
they were in a hurry and I stopped to see
who it was. There was a full moon and it
was a clear night. It was a man in a white
kitle, and with a paper cap on his head. He

came on without seeing me for I was standing in t' shadow of a wall. When he got near me the moonlight fell full upon his face and I saw that his mouth was swollen and cut, and that blood was oozing from it on one side. T' pocket of t' kitle was torn. It was torn in t' same way as t' pocket of t' kitle now produced. To the best of my belief it is one and t' same kitle. I recognized t' man. It was Mattha Tindale. I will swear it was. He got on t' top of t' wall, and when he saw me he just looked for a moment and then dropped over all in a hurry, and I heard him trampling through t' undergrowth as if he was afraid of me coming after him."

Mr. James Garod, the leading counsel for the defence here rose and cross-questioned the witness.

What was he doing that night in the Derthwaite woods? Nothing. Oh, indeed. Was there a footpath in that particular part where he had been? There was not. The learned counsel here remarked with a slightly

cynical smile, though with a gracious manner,
that he supposed the Derthwaite woods were
somewhat attractive; a remark which provoked suppressed laughter from the gods
who were aware of the witness's propensity.
Continuing, the counsel said he would like
to ask one more question. Was the witness
standing or crouching behind the wall, when,
as he affirmed, he saw the prisoner? He was
crouching. Then would the witness be good
enough to say why he was crouching?

All these questions the witness answered
hesitatingly, and with visible discomfort and
annoyance, greatly to the delight of those
in the crowd who took pleasure in seeing
another's chagrin; they felt they were getting
a better entertainment—more in exchange for
their physical discomfort, so to speak—than
they had bargained for, and they waxed almost
jovial and merry. But when the witness
was re-examined, there seemed less cause for
laughter.

" People often go where there's no footpath;

the landowners aren't very particular about Staneby. I sometimes go out for a walk in t' evenin' after my day's work is done. I don't walk all t' time; perhaps I may sit down and rest mysel and hev a pipe. I might hev been hevin' a pipe beside t' wall when I saw Mattha Tindale; I don't remember."

In one corner of the court a stout, middle-aged woman was standing. Her bonnet-strings were untied, and she kept moistening her lips with her tongue, and occasionally looking round with an expression that was distressed and vague. It could not be the heat of the court from which she suffered, for the temperature was kept low by the wind and sleet that blew against the windows; neither could it be from the pressure of the crowd, for it was not excessive where she stood. And yet suffering of some kind was plainly denoted by her face. There were two little horizontal lines between the eyebrows; and occasionally the eyelids closed, remaining in that position for so long that it almost seemed as if they desired to pass from a momentary respite in looking at the scene, to the more perfect rest of sleep. But sleep must have been far from the woman, for always at the end of two or three minutes the eyelids were lifted, and the eyes showed the light of perfect consciousness. She was very pale, but this might be her natural complexion. When she was not looking at the prisoner, she kept her eyes upon the judge, or the barristers engaged in the case; and it was curious to see how deepest shade fell upon her face, or winter sunlight, according to the direction which her eyes had taken. The pitiful expression of the mouth, the troubled, almost terror-stricken look in the eyes, the muscular fall of the cheeks, vanished when her head was turned toward the prisoner, so that nothing was seen of them. Nay, when their eyes met she would even smile; her lips trembled, but the distance between them perhaps hid this from the prisoner. The bravery of Spartan women is boasted of. English women are as brave as they.

Another witness quickly followed the shoemaker, and the crowd listened attentively.

"My name is John Addison. I am superintendent of police, and am stationed at Merton. In consequence of information received from the last witness, I went on Saturday, the 28th of November, to Staneby, in company with Police-sergeant Ritson and Police-constable Jackson. I drove direct to the smithy, where I found the prisoner at work. I then charged him with having caused the death of Mr. Sidney Aschenburg. He seemed in no way surprised or moved. I told him he might consider himself in custody, at the same time warning him to be careful what he said. For a few minutes he stood as if lost in thought, then he said, deliberately, 'I wish to make a statement to you. I had a deep grudge against Mr. Sidney Aschenburg—for he had done me the kind of injury a man does not easily get over—and

I set off, meaning to go to Derthwaite to see him, but I met him on the fisherman's path, and tackled him with it; and then I felt as if nothing would satisfy me but his life, and after a great struggle I threw him into the river, but I did not leave home meaning to kill him.'"

"Will you swear that he said 'a deep grudge,' and not 'grudge' merely?" asked Mr. James Garod, cross-examining.

"I swear he said 'a deep grudge.'"

"Will you swear that he said he did not leave home meaning to kill him?"

"I will swear it."

The woman in the corner of the court fixed her eyes intreatingly upon the barrister, but he sat down.

Here a narrow-faced, sandy-haired man, with a freckled complexion, was called into the witness-box, and some delay occurred through his asking if he could not tell the truth without 'kissing the book.'"

"Certainly, my friend," suavely put in the

counsel for the prosecution, an Irishman, who was of a jocular turn of mind. " Most of us hope, as honourable men, to be able to speak the truth without having to pass under the spell laid on us by kissing the book. However, the law in the present instance asks from you the favour of this little formality, unless, of course, your conscience forbids it."

The oath, however, was taken, and the witness said nervously, while he carefully weighed each sentence before allowing it to pass his lips—

" My [name is Timothy Dixon. I am a farmer, and rent Long Close from Sir William Garod. I have known Mattha Tindale for some years, and have always employed him to do my smithying. I remember the 27th of November. I went rather earlier than usual that night to the Garod Arms. I was there when Mattha Tindale came in. After he had been there a little while he got very excited, and I could see there was something on his mind that troubled him. And after a while he began and told us. He said that he had set off to go to Derthwaite to see Mr. Sidney Aschenburg. He had, however, met him on the fisherman's path. He said that he challenged Mr. Sidney Aschenburg to fight, and, seeing a small stick in his hand, he wrenched it from him, and threw it into the wood. He said they did not take off their coats when they fought; and that in the last struggle they had together, Mr. Sidney Aschenburg caught hold of his—Mattha Tindale's—kitle, and between them, one pulling one way and the other another way, it got torn. Some of us pressed him to tell what they had quarrelled about, but he refused. He told us he was mad with anger, and that he had made up his mind to have Mr. Sidney's life. He said he had not expected to see him till he got to Derthwaite. He then described the way in which they struggled, and how he had caught hold of Mr. Sidney Aschenburg's arms, and had gradually pressed him to the edge of the cliff, and then over into the river, for by this time he said he had made up his mind that he would have his life. He told us he had seen Neddy Kendal as he went home, and that Neddy was behind a wall."

Again Mr. James Garod rose to cross-examine, his straight, black eyebrows drawn together, and one hand carefully going round his shaven chin until it reached the small patch of whisker which extended an inch below his ear. His manner was not one to reassure witnesses "for the other side;" and Mr. Timothy Dixon turned away, hoping to escape being questioned through timely flight.

"One moment, my dear sir," began the barrister ; and the witness turned nervously back again, feeling as if those two half turns had made him quite giddy.

"There are one or two little things I would like to ask you. Was there much drinking at the Garod Arms on that particular night which you mention ? Not much. Then what was the cause of the prisoner's excitement before he began to tell you of his encounter with Mr. Sidney Aschenburg? Oh, indeed! Neddy Kendal and he had been quarrelling, that was it. Judging from what you have seen of the prisoner, would you say that he was of a quarrelsome disposition? You would say so; you've seen him very often quarrelling with people? Oh. A bad tempered man, in fact—one whom you should think very likely to be suddenly roused to a fit of uncontrollable anger? Oh, I see—really a passionate man. Did the prisoner tell you that he had a quarrel at any time with Mr. Sidney Aschenburg, or that he owed him a grudge? He never told you that? Only some of you—meaning, I suppose, some of the company at the inn— some of you thought that he must have had, or he would not have challenged him to fight? Oh, I see; that is how you came to think they must have had a quarrel, or that the prisoner owed Mr. Sidney Aschenburg a grudge—you just fancied it must be so? In fact, you made it up all out of your own heads, as the children say ? Thank you, I will not trouble you further."

But here the counsel for the prosecution rose hurriedly, and said he must detain the witness for a moment. And so Mr. Timothy Dixon was re-examined.

" I never saw the prisoner quarrel with any one but Neddy Kendal," answered the witness hesitatingly, and blinking very fast. as he looked nervously round the hall. " I never heard him say a wrong word to any one else ; and I never heard him say. a wrong word to Neddy very often. Some people, indeed, might say it was always as much Neddy's fault as Mattha Tindale's. Neddy Kendal was at times very nasty to Mattha—in fact, he was very nasty the night that Mattha told about what he had done to Mr. Sidney Aschenburg. No, I don't think I should say that Mattha was a quarrelsome or a passionate man. It was that gentleman opposite that somehow made me say so. Mattha told us that he would never tell what he and Mr.

Sidney Aschenburg had quarrelled about, and that it was a secret which only he and Mr. Sidney Aschenburg knew."

After this a light cane was produced, and sworn to as having been found in the quarry wood above the Devil's Pot, at a distance of about fifty yards from the scene where it had been asserted the struggle between the prisoner and Mr. Sidney Aschenburg took place. The cane was identified by a servant from Derthwaite as one which had been in the possession of his late master.

This closed the case for the prosecution.

Mr. James Garod said that he would only call witnesses as to character.

Robert Fawcett, yeoman, of Seatenner, was first called. He said that he had known the prisoner for many years, and had always respected him as a good and conscientious workman. He had always found him a man of high moral character, and, from what he knew of him, he should not consider him of a revengeful nature.

Evidence of a similar kind was given by the vicar of Staneby.

There was a slight pause, and the woman in the corner of the court knowing who was to speak next for the prisoner, flushed with a sudden feverish heat, paling as quickly, while she began to tremble from head to foot as if an ague had seized her. All morning she had been longing for the time when this witness should be questioned ; and yet now that he was coming she dreaded to hear the sound of his voice. Supposing, she asked herself—supposing he should not say the right things ; or supposing he should not say them in the right way, what then ? And for the first time that day, her eyes, filled with their hopeless misery, were turned upon the prisoner: the man had been her stay always and comfort ever since the time when he had played at her feet a little white-haired boy; and it was so natural a thing to go to him when in trouble, that for the moment her dire distress rose to the extinction of the memory of his sorrow, and she turned her face to his.

He, however, did not see it, for his eyes were no longer fixed on that corner of the court, but were shifting, with the close observant looks that are sometimes turned on trivial objects when the mind is over-strained, from the statue of Mercy on one side of the judge to that of Justice on the other, and so backward and forward as though comparing the attributes of each. It seemed just then as if he were paying no attention to what was going on around him. Not for an instant were his eyes lowered to the grave self-possessed looking man who was entering the witness-box, and who a few seconds later confronted the examining barrister with a demeanour as calm and indicative of hidden strength as his own. And yet all the while his ears were strained to catch every sound.

The witness said, " My name is George Hodgson. I am the senior partner in the firm of Hodgson, Brackenrigg and Scatterbeck, solicitors, practising at Merton. I have known the prisoner six months. I first saw him in August last when he came to our offices. The business he then entrusted to me was of so extraordinary a nature, that my curiosity was awakened concerning him, and instead of passing the case on to one of the other members of the firm, which is usually my habit when a client is personally unknown to me, I determined to keep it in my own hands. The prisoner was legally possessed of property which, for a man of his social position, was considerable; yet he did not think in equity that the property could be his, persons being, as he believed, alive who had a prior claim. He therefore instructed me to enter upon a systematic endeavour to find them by the ordinary, but expensive, advertising mediums, telling me that he wished to transfer the property to them. On my remarking that I supposed the expenses would be paid out of the estate, I was told with some show of warmth, that his savings were to pay all the necessary costs, for he was determined that those who had been kept out of the property, which he considered should have been theirs thirty years ago, should not find that it had been lessened when at length it came into their hands. These instructions I carried out; he paying me at fairly regular intervals, sums varying from ten to fifteen pounds. He paid me in all for advertising, sixty-three pounds. When the last instalment was paid, he told me that his savings were spent, and that now the advertising must only be done, as he expressed it, from hand to mouth; that is to say, as small sums were realized by him they would be laid out in advertisements."

Here the papers necessary to prove the validity of Matthew Tindale's claim upon the estate in question, were put in as evidence. Also vouchers for the payment of the advertisements; and the day-book of the firm of Hodgson, Brackenrigg and Scatterbeck, solicitors, proving that payment of certain sums for advertising had been made by the prisoner.

The examination of Mr. George Hodgson was then continued. He said, "I have been in practice five and thirty years as a solicitor, and have never known of a case in which a man under similar conditions, has wished and endeavoured to give up property to others, believing those others to have a prior claim, in equity, to himself. I believe the case is unique. Men usually come to me to have their grasp tightened upon property—occasionally to try to get what is not legally theirs; but never, save in this solitary case, has any man come to me, saying he wished to give up to others property which was legally his own. The property is now in the hands of the Court of Chancery. This was done by request of the prisoner, a week after the examination before the magistrates."

While this evidence was being given, the delicate forefinger of the judge worked thoughtfully round two deep wrinkles which rose in a transverse line across the corners of his mouth, and his eyes looked keenly at the witness. It was a curious recital ; and, moving the delicate forefinger, he made some notes hastily on the sheet of paper before him. He had glanced at the prisoner before looking down at the paper. He had half expected to see the man draw himself up a little, and perhaps even look round at the court to mark the effect of the evidence. But no, there was no change ; the same quiet, unostentatious demeanour ; no expression was increased or lessened.

Then the counsel for the prosecution rose to cross-examine.

The witness said, "I had no reason for doubting the existence of those persons for whom my client advertised. Men do not usually spend sixty-three pounds upon a phantom of their brain."

Here there was a murmur of applause, which was instantly hushed.

Continuing, the witness said, "My client bore a feeling of resentment toward the

testator for the injury he believed him to have
done to those whom he considered should have
had the property; but I never heard him utter
a word of personal resentment—resentment
arising from a feeling of having been personally
injured by the testator unwittingly laying upon
him this burden of finding the rightful owner
of the property."

Re-examined by Mr. James Garod, the
witness said, " I always found the prisoner to
have peculiarly strict notions of honour. I
found he was a man likely to be roused to
anger by the knowledge of any deed of wrong.
I have seen evidence of hastiness of temper in
him, but never any signs of brooding passion."

The jury was then addressed for the prosecution. The learned counsel said that any
question of the prisoner having thrown the
deceased over the cliff, either in self-defence or
by accident, the struggle having taken place
upon the edge of a cliff over-hanging a river,
or in a fit of sudden anger, could not be enter-
tained. He dwelt at great length on the state-

ment made by the prisoner when charged. Also he pointed out the fact that no attempt had been made by the prisoner to avail himself of the opportunities that had occurred of making any statement that would set up a defence to the accusation. What was the grudge, the existence of which they had such ample proof? In the counsel's opinion, the evidence all tended to prove that there was no sudden and violent provocation on the part of the deceased, but that the crime had been committed with malice aforethought, and was, therefore, murder.

The prosecuting counsel having spoken for nearly an hour, sat down. He was immediately followed by Mr. James Garod for the defence.

CHAPTER II.

THE TRIAL—*Continued.*

THE counsel for the defence could plead well, and was fully aware of his power. Trusting alone to the force of his manner and delivery, and to the musical tones of his voice, he went through his speech, disdaining any gesture, saving a backward throw of the head, a quick turning of it from side to side, with a fierce, unreturnable glance of the dark eyes.

As he spoke, the woman in the corner of the court watched him eagerly. In place of the unhealthy glow as of a fever, which at one time had run through her veins, a natural and spontaneous warmth began to spread itself, and, like generous wine, it drove the colour over her cheeks, and brought animation to her eyes. What were those words to which she was listening? Were ever such brave and good and true ones said? Surely, every one now must see that the man for whom they were spoken was a noble man, in spite of the deed he had done, and would be able to understand as did she, how it had all come about that he was there that day as a prisoner before them. He was making it very clear. How simple it all seemed when he came to speak. She had been told that it would go hard with the man who was standing his trial for life, because he had a grudge against him whom he had smitten to his death. And she had rebelled against such a saying. It had seemed strange that what to her was a kind of excuse—if excuse can ever be made for wrong doing—should prove his condemnation. But she was growing quite easy about the issue; indeed, she felt almost happy, for this gentleman spoke as if he understood everything well, and knew just

how to put it. Even now when he was talking
about the law, a thing which usually puzzled
her very much, she could follow him, at least
she could listen to his long sentences. She was
glad he said some very learned things, because
she was sure this also would tell in favour of
the prisoner.

And Matthew, how was it with him?

The long weary hours during which he had
stood in the dock had drooped his frame a
little. His hands were laid on the wood-work
before him, and it seemed, if one could judge
by the pressure of his fingers, as though the
weight of the shoulders was being put upon
them. He, like the woman. in the corner
of the court, was listening to every word
spoken by the counsel. But he was differently
affected by it. How poor, how trivial it all
seemed. If he only might have spoken up for
himself, and pleaded for his deed in his own
rough fashion, would it not have been better.
Would not his heart have burned, and words,
simple it is true and unlearned, but still

brightening up and glowing with the fire in
his heart, have been poured out filled with
truer eloquence than this man's ? The words
to which he was listening were gradually
chilling him and driving away hope. They
were but the fine words of a gentleman,
backed by no feeling, and spoken as though
they were dropped out at the rate of so many
per hour. If he only might have spoken, how
he would have told the jury and the people in
that court of fair-seeming things, such as
tender kisses, and honeyed words; and then of
a betrayal, and finally of the casting aside of a
devotion whose only shame was that it had
been too great. How he would have told
them—and his lips would have trembled with
passionate eagerness—of his sister's purity ; he
would have spoken of her in such terms, that
the very roof would have rung with cries of
shame upon her destroyer. The crowd would
have yelled at last, that the deed must be con-
doned for the sake of the mighty wrong that
called it forth ; that vengeance was a fit thing

to see in a brother's hand, and that even if the
crime were great, it should be weighed with
other crimes, and regarded as lying less
heavily in the balance because of the provocation he had received. But then—Matthew
checked himself suddenly. No such defence
as this could be made. He kept the secret of
that grudge which had stood between himself
and the dead man ; had kept it in spite of all
pressure which had been put upon him from
without, for his sister's sake. How could he
have borne to see her there in court, telling,
on his behalf, the story of her shame ? How
could he have borne to have heard her
questioned by the men there—his timid gentle
sister—concerning her love and her betrayal ?
No, it seemed to him that it would be easier
to die, far easier ; and he closed his eyes as
if to banish sight. Here his attention went
back to the speech which the counsel for the
defence was making. And he began wondering again what ailed it. Had he been skilled
in formulating ideas and clothing them in

words, he might perhaps have said, that it was because the very soul had been taken out of the history of the encounter between himself and Mr. Sidney Aschenburg by the withholding the cause of the quarrel, and that but a lifeless puppet had been placed in the hands of the counsel, so it was not to be wondered at that he could only give it a semblance of life, and could by no means make it appear to live, and move, and breathe.

And yet a death-like silence hung over the court, and an electric feeling of suspense communicated itself from one to another, as the counsel now poured out a torrent of impassioned words, his voice beating upon the air with curious vibrating thrills, now pleaded in sentences that seemed—for it was art this *seeming*, words coming swiftly to James Garod —as though they toiled after each other laboriously while his voice failed. He had thrown the spell of his eloquence over all his hearers, saving upon the judge and upon the prisoner. The former was listening to it impassionately and admiring it as a piece of art; the latter was considering what it lacked. Others there were, members of the bar, upon whom the spell would break with the closing word, and who would then immediately pass into the judge's frame of mind, but for the time they were caught and carried away by the bearing of the speaker, by the tones of his voice, by the magnificent skill with which he emphasized this sentence, and lightly, as with a touch of down, passed over that. He paused once, but this was only for effect, and then before the sympathic link existing between speaker and hearer could be broken, he went on again, saying—·

"You have been asked, gentlemen, by my learned friend to consider the meaning of the words 'malice aforethought,' and you have had several passages read to you, bearing upon constructions which may be put upon those words. Now, I dare say some of you will feel, after listening to the very able and subtile arguments which were then used, that

I am setting myself a difficult task when I tell you, that I hope to prove incontestibly how slight is the evidence upon which 'malice aforethought' can be urged against this man; nay, I will even go further, and say that there is no evidence. If you will favour me with your attention, I hope in a few minutes to be able to prove this to you. No witness— pray mark this, for it is an important fact— has been called in the case for the prosecution to give evidence relating either to words or actions on the part of this man, which could prove that he was plotting the death of the deceased. No witness has said, I heard the prisoner say he would be revenged upon him, or that he would bring about his death, or if he met him it would be the worse for him, or a like phrase. We are not told that on a given day, *before* that on which deceased met his death, this man said he owed the deceased a grudge, or the deceased had wronged him. Thus we have no direct evidence of this man brooding revengefully upon some supposed or actual insult, injury, or quarrel received from or existing between himself and the deceased. Turning to the evidence given by some of the witnesses for the prosecution, we find two of them making certain statements, upon which I venture to suppose my learned friend bases the charge against this man of malice afore-thought. I propose dealing with the evidence of each witness separately. We will first take into consideration that of Timothy Dixon. Now Timothy Dixon never tells us distinctly and clearly that this man on the night in question, at the Garod Arms, said he had a grudge against the deceased. What he tells us is, that he and others then present in the inn, thought there must have been a quarrel of some kind which had led to the struggle on the edge of the cliff, and that they pressed this man to tell them about it. He refused to answer them. Now mark this—my learned friend says, from the very fact of this man's silence, there is a tacit acknowledgment of a grudge, of a brooding revenge. Now will you hear me, and consider what I have to say upon this silence. I maintain that if this man had borne a grudge against the deceased, an inveterate hatred which craved for satisfaction, he would at once have told of it, there and then, in the presence of his neighbours and comrades as an excuse, a reason, a plea for the deed of which he stood, so it is asserted, self-accused. He would have wanted to palliate that which he said he had done ; he would have wanted to excuse the offence in their eyes ; for which of us will not testify that we love to stand well with our fellowmen, and that we will offer anything in extenuation for a particular action, rather than suffer the loss of their approbation and esteem ? Is not the respect of those around us a kind of moral sunshine in which we love to bask ? the hero of a hundred battles stands under the heat of its meridian splendour ; but with us, that vast majority unknown to fame, it shines with a soft benignity which comforts and cheers as we toil through the working day. Tell me not that this man is heedless of the entrancing warmth of that sunshine; that to him, the honour and respect of men, the homage and regard of women, is as nothing. With us he shares a common humanity which craves, no matter in how many other things it may be diverse, to stand before men esteemed and honoured. Thus I claim that he should be released from the charge of that grudge. Had it existed, he would have caught at it, have held it up, have made the most of it, have exaggerated its proportions; instead of that we find that he holds his peace. We have no hint even of such a thing having existed, as this fit of brooding revenge, of which the learned counsel has made so much, in the evidence put before us by Timothy Dixon. And now let us consider the evidence given by the Superintendent of Police. He says on oath, that this man stated to him that he had 'a deep grudge' against Mr. Sidney Aschen-burg. This statement, made thirty-six hours after this man had been badgered on all sides

230   MATTHEW TINDALE.

to make a confession of some old-standing
quarrel, does not appear to me to be of much
value in the case for the prosecution.   We all
know how easy a thing it is to drop the seed
of suspicion into a man's mind, even when
the seed is to grow up against himself.
Let the mind of a man be in an excited
condition, and suggest to him a course of
thought which you say in your opinion has
actuated him in the committal of such and
such a deed, and, in ninety-nine cases out
of a hundred, that man will come to think
with you, and will even be prepared to state
on oath that the train of emotional experience
you suggest was actually that which led him to
commit the deed.   Let us take a very homely
illustration of this psychological fact.   Have
none of you been told at any time that you
have done or said this or that—a thing which
at once you emphatically deny ; but upon the
charge being repeated you begin to doubt
the evidence of your own memory, until you
feel uncertain and wavering ; when finally the

idea becomes fixed with you that your first
impression was wrong, and that you have said
or done the thing with which you have been
charged? I think most of us will say that
this is not an uncommon experience; that
there have been many times, indeed, in which
we have yielded to the persuasion of others,
until at last we believed ourselves to have done
the very things of which at one time we held
ourselves innocent. Now, let me in my turn
drop a thought into your minds, which I
would ask you to consider seriously. May
not such an experience as I have endeavoured
rudely to lay before you have come to this
man? Can you not for yourselves imagine the
great mental strain put upon him between the
night at the Garod Arms and the next day,
when a certain charge was made against him
as he worked in his forge? and can you not
imagine that mental strain resulting in an
unhealthy condition of the brain, whereby any
thought entering upon it, just at that particular time, would be liable to perversion,

especially if that thought could be united to and form part of the sequence of thought which was the cause of the mental over-strain? If we in simple matters readily fall victims to suggestions made to us by others, how much more readily would this man, whose mind, as I have striven to show you, must have been in an abnormal condition— a condition unusual with him—have come under the influence of that questioning to which he had been subjected. If we begin to doubt the evidence of our own memories when a charge is made repeatedly against us, how much more would this man, whose mental frame was distracted and over-wrought. How those words uttered by his comrades would get at last to ring in his ears; how the questions would repeat themselves, until he would grow half mad with the reiteration; how by degrees he would yield to their per-sistency, until at length he would come to believe what had been suggested to him was possible, and that perhaps after all he had

had some old quarrel, some long-harboured grudge against the deceased; and finally the thought would find favour with him, for it would seem so much more reasonable, so much more excusable, that revenge for some pique should have prompted the struggle, than that a sudden and mad fit of passion should be put forward as an excuse for his deed. And so the old love of desiring to stand well before his fellow-men would come out surreptitiously, and, seeking marriage with this new belief, would strengthen it until, the thought taking a fast hold, the idea of a brooding revenge would pass from the shadowy regions of imagination into the world of accomplished facts. I would plead with you seriously to consider what I have been endeavouring to put before you, and, for the reasons given, not too readily to take the statement literally, which you are told on oath was made by this man. You will then be able to ask with me, Where is the evidence of this long-stored grudge? Where are the signs

that it ever existed before the day on which
the deceased met his death? By what evidence is it that we are asked to believe that
this man set out with the malice aforethought
in his heart, which was to bring death to his
victim? A few more words and I have done
with the evidence laid before you by the
learned counsel for the prosecution; but these
few words I would say with all the impres-
siveness which lies at my command. If one
sentence of the statement made by this man
when formally charged by the superintendent
of police has been thought worthy of being
held up to your notice, we must not overlook
the fact that there is another sentence far
more noteworthy, if we take into consideration
the evidence which goes to support it. It is
this—and, mark you, it has been given and
repeated under oath—that this man said he
did not leave home intending to kill the
deceased. Does not this agree with what we
have been told of the character of this man?
Is it likely that one of high moral rectitude,

of generous purpose, of strict notions of honour, should carry within his breast the base and cruel and wicked desire that seeks gratification in the death of any one? We have been told a story relating to him which must have caused every generous impulse we possessed to glow and burn. It is a rare thing, as my friend Mr. Hodgson said, to find a man giving up property which he could legally claim—so rare a thing, that I have never heard a case like that which has been put before us to-day, in any of the many courts which it has been my business and privilege to attend. And yet we are asked to believe that this man, who stripped himself of every sovereign he possessed; who worked over hours, early in the morning and late at night, that he might give unsparingly of the labour of his hands, for the benefit of persons whom he had never seen, and of whose very existence he was not sure, simply because he believed them to have been wronged; we are asked, I say, to believe that this man was yet carrying with him the desire, the fierce thirst which longed to slake itself in a vengeance of blood. I ask you, do the two things agree? Could the man who was known as a good neighbour, an honest, upright, and conscientious workman, whose character up to the fatal day was unimpeachable; could this man, I say, be guilty of a crime born of malice and maliciously put into execution? Could he have gone about his daily avocations, rising early and working late from noble love of righting what he deemed a wrong; could he have been the good neighbour, the true and honest workman, mindful of the money and time of his employers as of his own; courteous and considerate to all he met; could he, I repeat, have been all this, and carried at the same time so damnable a purpose in his heart? Surely this man spoke the truth when he said he did not leave home intending to bring about the death of the deceased. This statement agrees with what we have been told of his character. Surely he went out, and meeting

Mr. Sidney Aschenburg, words passed between them which resulted in a quarrel that unhappily terminated fatally for one of the persons engaged, no fell purpose having possessed the other. He had gone out; his temper had been roused, and in a sudden fit of passion he hurled his adversary into the river. There was no one to witness the terrible struggle. No one, who can come here and tell us how the two swayed backward and forward toward that fatal precipice. The evidence which has been laid before us brings us up to this point, and then there is a sudden breaking of the thread—neither you nor I nor any one can tell how that struggle went; whether at times it would have appeared that it was now this one who desired to push the other over, and now that. Passions lie deep-seated within the human heart. Which of us therefore dare rise up in judgment and say that in this man they were quickened into a terrible intensity which worked to a fatal end, while in that of the dead man they were quiescent. Which of us will venture to be judge between them? Which of us will venture to say, the one had murderous intentions in his heart, while the other was free from all thought of crime? The balance hangs equally. In the eyes of men, if one man be guilty, the other must be guilty too. If one be innocent of any intention of crime, then to the other innocence must be imputed too. Look at the figures of Justice and Mercy which stand on either side of the judge! Let the gentle leniency of the one fall upon your hearts, and all the sterner qualities of her sister will unite themselves with it. In mercy you will find the truest justice—justice may be severed from mercy, but mercy locks her hands in those of justice. I ask you therefore fearlessly for a verdict of acquittal. I ask you to set free, the true, the good, the noble workman; to send back to his home to-day this man, whose character it has been shown to us, is fair and spotless but for this one shadow. I plead with you, that to-morrow's sun may rise and find him free. I plead that the upland valley may once more give him foot-hold, her erring and yet—who can gainsay it?—her truly noble son. It is with confidence I trust his fate to you; with confidence I leave it in your hands."

The counsel for the defence broke off abruptly; but even this abrupt termination had been calculated upon, and was part of James Garod's art. People were startled by it, and for a few minutes a silence born of yet deeper suspense prevailed. Then there came a faint rustle of movement, and the drawing as of one deep breath of relief passing through the hall. Would the prisoner be acquitted? and each looked into the eyes of his neighbour with the question unasked upon his lips.

The woman in the corner of the hall was smiling and pressing forward as far as she could for the crowd. But the prisoner was standing with his head slightly drooping as though very weary, and his eyes fixed on his hands which, grasping the bar of the dock, seemed as if they were now bearing the full weight of his shoulders. To one the counsel's address had been full of the promise of life; to the other of the promise of death.

Then the judge in a thin, high, unimpassioned voice proceeded to sum up, and once more perfect stillness fell upon the hall.

He asked the jury to dismiss from their minds the possible consequence of their verdict, and to strive so far as possible to prevent any feeling of sentiment actuating them in the discharge of their duty. The prisoner had been charged with murder, and the case was an unusually painful one, owing to the high moral character which, up to the time of the fatal occurrence, the prisoner had borne. With regard to the law of the matter, all killing of another person by another was *prima facie* murder, and the question they had to decide was whether the offence the prisoner had committed was murder or something less. Murder was the killing of another with malice aforethought; manslaughter was the killing of another, there being no question of malice aforethought in the constitution of the crime. When there had been provocation, and a sufficient time for passion to subside and reason to interpose, and yet the person so provoked afterwards killed the other, this was deliberate revenge, and accordingly amounted to murder. If, on the other hand, a man had been greatly provoked and immediately killed the aggressor, the law paid that regard to human frailty, as not to put a hasty act upon the same footing as that of a deliberate one; and although the act was inexcusable, since there was no absolute necessity for doing it, yet it was not murder, for there was no previous malice, but it was manslaughter. Hence, manslaughter was the unlawfully killing of another without premeditation; and murder was the unlawfully killing of another with malice aforethought, either expressed or implied. The question which they had to consider was whether the prisoner with premeditated purpose killed Sidney Aschenburg. The judge pointed out that they had been asked on evidence of the slenderest character to acquit the prisoner altogether. He left it to the jury to say whether they were satisfied of there being evidence of an old grudge between the parties; if they were satisfied they would no doubt find him guilty of murder. If, on the contrary, they believed that the evidence pointed toward a sudden quarrel on the meeting of the prisoner with the deceased, and that there was no time for passion to cool and reason to gain dominion over the mind, they would no doubt find him guilty of manslaughter only. The judge then entered into an exhaustive review of the evidence, and, in conclusion, warned the jury not to return a verdict of murder unless they were absolutely certain of malice aforethought having actuated the prisoner.

The jury then retired, and the silence which

had again hung over the court during the judge's address was exchanged for the sound of faint rustlings, uneasy movements of impatient feet, coughs which had been checked, the subdued murmuring of voices, all the signs that tell of the withdrawal of a feeling of interested suspense, and the incoming one of impatience against a time that will be heavy for want of diversion. Those in the crowd who had come to watch the proceedings from a love of law had lost their interest in the case, for they knew which way the verdict must turn, but they did not endeavour to edge their way out of the crowd; they had waited so long, and might as well wait for the end. Those whose nature caused them to find a fiendish enjoyment in the torture of others, were waiting with hungry impatience for what they fondly hoped would prove to be the most appetising bite of all. They spoke in whispers to their neighbours, and what they said provoked muffled laughter, and caused their eyes to gleam curiously. While those,

upon whose minds civilization worked her
charms but feebly, and whose emotions, be-
gotten of the scene which had been enacted
before them, had "thrown back" to some
ape-like progenitor, crimson-lipped with the
blood of his own race, stood with a burning fire running through their veins, while
their hands clasped and unclasped each
other, as though it were necessary to keep
them fast bound lest they too should strike
out, as they longed to do, and slay a man.
The woman's face in the far corner of the
court changed to a deathly hue, and her knees
smote one upon another and shook; and her
hands turned cold and clammy, and she
seemed as if about to faint. And the prisoner
watched her, as with head held up and hands
that no longer sought support, he strove to
pierce the shadows that the lamps, which for
the last two hours had filled the court with a
yellow misty glow, yet failed to dissipate.
He moved uneasily, as if he would have gone
to her but for the barrier that held him in.

and then he looked round upon the faces of the crowd, as if he would mutely implore some help for her.

When at last the jury returned, there was no need to impose silence, for the crowd, from various motives, desired it for its own sake.

The calling over of the names of the jury-men occupied a few minutes; after which the regulation question was put and answered before the final one, which was to seal the prisoner's doom.

"Gentlemen of the jury, have you agreed upon your verdict?"

"We have."

"Do you find the prisoner guilty or not?"

"We find the prisoner guilty of murder, but strongly recommend him to mercy."

A low cry came from that corner of the court where the woman stood. And there was a movement and an endeavour to raise something which had slipped to the ground. And there was a pressure and striving amongst the crowd, and something was slowly and with

difficulty dragged through it toward one of
the doorways. And a whisper, "It is his
mother," was passed on from one to another,
until it found its way to the barristers, and
finally to the judge.

The judge paused ; for there is a sorrow
before which all must hold themselves
reverently, even as in the presence of
death.

At the sound of that cry Matthew drew
himself up quickly, every muscle braced and
held as firmly as in the days of old. He laid
hold of the barrier, and it seemed for a moment
as if he were about to vault over it ; but
restraining hands were instantly put out.
Before, however, they could touch his, he had
checked himself, saying apologetically to those
who stood around—

"I forgot. But you'll understand it was
but natural I should want to go to her."

And then to Matthew there was a confused
babel of sound, which was, however, in reality
but that of one unimpassioned, high, thin

voice. And the lights in the court became dim. His thought had followed the woman who had been carried out ; and, saving for the scene which his imagination pictured, he was deaf and blind.

CHAPTER III.

WE REAP WHAT ANOTHER HAS SOWN.

IT was the day after the trial.

The wind still blew keenly, and hail-showers swept over the terrace at Derthwaite, lashing the gravel and pitting holes in the soil of the empty flower-beds. Cold gleams of sunshine came at intervals between the clouds, shining upon the tiny pools of water which stood in place of the hailstones, and on the blades of grass which trembled and flickered in the wind, and upon the glistening laurel bushes and yew hedges in the shrubbery. The smoke from the chimneys which rose at regular intervals from Derthwaite, was blown now swiftly in a long straight line, now turned and twisted about and beaten low down against the red sandstone roofing, then for a brief moment allowed to rise in a thin grey tremulous column, only to be caught again and whirled about and scattered before the wind. Juno was lying in her kennel in the yard, her nose resting upon her outstretched fore-legs, her nostrils twitching uneasily, while her brown eyes rested on the pool of water which was gradually increasing in length and width in front of her kennel; she lifted up her head to growl when the hail came and splashed into the tiny pond, but relapsed into a wakeful silence so soon as it ceased. There had been a time when she had been almost always on the alert, seemingly waiting for some one; now, however, the fancy must have passed from her, for she no longer leaped up restlessly and bounded to the length of her chain at the sound of every distant step. And in her loose-box, Harkaway munched her oats, too warm and comfortable to be mindful of the gusts outside, which whirled the ventilator at a speed that caused odd creakings and groanings to come from the stable roof. Beyond on the moor, where she used to gallop with her young master, white-breasted sea-birds were swooping down here and there, to rise with fierce wild cries, until they were lost against the grey wind-driven clouds ; the brown heather was shaking and trembling, and the drops of moisture that clung to the stunted trees that grew in the boundary hedges, had to fall ere they could be turned by the wintry sun into bright glisten-ing jewels.

A cold cheerless day, and yet below the terrace at Derthwaite, and beyond the walks that turned and twisted about in the shrubbery, where a narrow path led from the wicket that opened upon the meadows up to some wide-spreading yews, Frances Carter walked. Thick furs were round her throat ; a close-fitting hat defied the gusts of wind ; and some strong woollen material covered her from shoulder to foot and protected her from the hail.

In the four months which had elapsed since Sidney Aschenburg's death, her face had changed a little; its curves were less rounded, and the colour which used to be so bright and fresh had paled. There had grown into her face a look which told of a nature enriched, added to, and built up. Such a look as this comes with maternity; it comes also when a vast love supplies the arc which makes the broken circle of existence complete—these are two of the sunny things which bring it; but it may come with the shadows, if the nature on which the shadows fall be noble and deeply receptive. This was how it had come to Frances Carter. Her forehead was unruffled, and a great calm had fallen upon it and upon her eyes, and a strength which was new to them had lighted upon her lips, a strength which told, however, of the baptism of pain. One felt in looking at her, that some cataclysm had swept over her, which had broken up all that is stiff and unyielding in girl-nature, and that the fountain of what is sweet and rich was unsealed, and that she had passed from girlhood into a womanhood that would gradually open into a perfect and glorious maturity. The Frances Carter who was pacing that narrow path was not the same Frances who had come to Derthwaite six months before; then there had only been the fairness of promise, now there was the richness of fulfilment.

The hail had fallen intermittently, little heeded by Frances; but a more violent shower than before drove her to find shelter beneath the thick growth of a yew tree. She stood with her arms and hands folded within the woollen wrap, watching abstractedly the hail-stones as they danced on the sloping banks, now comparatively dry, or as they lay in tiny heaps that would melt before the next shower came. As she stood under the yew-tree, the dull eyes and the delicate transparency of the skin where it was shadowed by the eyelashes, told of something more than of her sorrow at Sidney's death; they told of the doubts and the perplexities that had fallen upon her, and which

during the past few days had reached a cul-
minating point. She had been called from
Florence, in case her presence should be required at the trial as the last person who, as
it was supposed, apart from Matthew had seen
Sidney Aschenburg alive. Frances herself
knew differently, and so did old Abel the nurse,
and it was what lay beneath this knowledge
that had caused the doubts and perplexities.

When the news was sent to her at Florence
of the way in which Sidney Aschenburg had
actually come by his death, and the name of
the man who had confessed to the deed, a hot
thrill passed through her, something wholly
apart from the horror called up by the act of
murder, and from the feeling of revulsion
against this self-accused murderer of her lover.
Instantly she lived again, as one who drowning lives through his life in a moment of time,
the scene enacted in the corridor outside
Sidney Aschenburg's room on the afternoon
preceding his death. She saw the girl who
had intercepted her path, her arms flung out,

her cheeks flaming, her eyes glaring like some
wild creature's whose lair has been discovered
by the huntsman, as she spoke cruel words
which fell from her with the weight of iron.
And she remembered the name by which the
girl called herself—the same name as that of
the man who accused himself of being Sidney
Aschenburg's murderer.   And then Frances
filled in the gaps of the story, the scenes which
her imagination conjured up seeming to her as
real as that one in which she herself had taken
part.   She pictured the girl enraged with
jealousy and shame, pouring out her story to
her brother, and awakening in him such anger
as would drive him out upon the errand which
worked the death of the betrayer.

The girl's story was true then—Sidney had
led a village maiden astray.   Hitherto it had
lacked the confirmation of common talk or the
laying openly of such a charge, and Frances by
degrees had learned to put aside the recollection of all that had been said to her that
evening in the corridor.   But when the

brother of the girl who had pronounced herself deceived by Sidney Aschenburg, confessed to having thrown him over the cliff, saying at the same time he had a grudge against him, Frances could no longer take to herself this slender comfort. And she wept often and bitterly.

Then, as time passed, one thought had practically to be grappled with.

The letters which went from Derthwaite to Florence, spoke repeatedly of the grudge which the man who charged himself with Sidney's death had spoken of as a pretext for the crime. They contained scornful references to it, and repeated assurances of the impossibility of a quarrel of any kind having existed between the young squire and the blacksmith. Then a letter came which said that village gossip had busied itself in giving out that the quarrel, grudge, or whatever it was had arisen about pretty Bella Hind, the yeoman's daughter, whom it was thought the blacksmith was courting, a suggestion which Mrs. Aschenburg rejected with scorn—so at least

she said in her letter.   But the next time she
wrote, and still lingering upon the subject as if
it were a fascinating one, she said that people
were even yet talking nonsense about Bella
Hind and her poor lost boy ; although the girl
herself had given a most emphatic contradic-
tion to the story, while not denying that she
had been the sweetheart of the man now in
custody.   But in this letter there were fewer
signs of the writer's being assured of the im-
probability of the tale ; she merely remarked
that if such a thing as a *liaison* between her
boy and a village girl had really taken place,
and the girl's sweetheart had avenged himself
in the way gossips would have her believe,
it was strange nothing had been said of it
before the magistrates, when, though she knew
nothing of law, it seemed to her that the man
would have been glad to have put forward the
plea of jealousy as an excuse for his crime ;
instead of which he had persistently kept
silence upon the subject of the quarrel, saying
that it was his own affair and no one's else.

After this, though Mrs. Aschenburg never directly referred to the story about Bella Hind and her son, Frances found from the tenor of her letters that she accepted it. Once she said, " I suppose jealousy will be put forward at the trial in the hope of obtaining a verdict of man-slaughter. In that case I must make up my mind to bear the bringing into light of many painful details." At another time, "I am coming myself gradually to the belief that jealousy was the cause of the crime." And then in another letter, and quite abruptly, as though after pausing with her pen in mid-air her thoughts had wandered from the subject on which she had been writing, " I suppose men quarrel to the death over the women they love—I am compelled to believe this barbarous dictum." And again, as if her thoughts went readily into some well-known tract, " His sister went away, so I am told— I mean the sister of the man who is to under-go his trial—she went away just at the very time he confessed to the deed at the Garod

Arms. How wise of her—I hear she has gone to a situation ; I wish we could all do as she has done and so escape the shame."

Thus the knowledge that Frances possessed of the interview she knew to have taken place, between the sister of the man who was waiting his trial and Sidney Aschenburg, began to weigh upon her. Could it be, she asked herself, that with the exception of the Tindales, she alone knew of the intimacy which had existed between the two—for with a strong intuitive knowledge she rejected the idea of a *liaison* between her lover and Bella Hind—and that this intimacy had been the cause of the crime? Almost it seemed to her that it must be so, for village gossip had never once brought forward Maggie Tindale's name. And what if any words that she could say would palliate the man's crime! And what if they could cause a verdict of manslaughter to be given instead of murder! Would she be justified in keeping back those words? And yet how could she stand in an open court and deliberately bear witness to the falsity of the man who, had he lived, would have been her husband? Did not all his faults cry out to her for pity, and seek a covering up at her hands?

And a faint echoing voice whispered out the words, " In some far-distant time, if follies and sins are attributed to me, will it change your love. Promise me that through good report and ill report I shall have your trust—if in the time to come there is no one to speak for me, no one to excuse me, no one to say ' He meant well,' will you stand up for me as though I were your husband ? "

The hail beat through the highest branches of the yew-tree beneath which Frances was sheltering, and a few of the white dancing things, round and uninjured, fell at her feet. But she did not see them, her thoughts were busy with the verdict that had been given the day before. Although summoned to England in case her presence should be required at the trial, it had been agreed later that it was unnecessary to put her to the pain of giving evidence as to her last interview with Sidney, therefore, she had not been in court during the proceedings, but Mr. Aschenburg had given her an account of much that had been done and said.

And as she stood beneath that yew-tree, it seemed to her as if she had taken upon herself the burden of the sacrifice of a man's life.

"As though you were my husband," she whispered, her lips trembling, and the sweet grey eyes that were now lifted to the patch of sky that appeared beyond the branches of the yew-tree filled with tears. "Beloved, I could not go against you, we are one in this sorrow ; you have borne your part, and now it passes to me. I cannot—oh, I cannot charge you, and together we will keep the secret of this pain, you dead and I living. I must shield you—as though—nay, for you *are* my husband."

The tears slowly dried in her eyes ; but

her face grew paler and though her lips closed firmly, their expression grew more sad. The wave of retribution following upon another's sin had caught her, that wave whose undulations were to play for ever through her life.

The hail-shower ceased, and the pale sunshine quickly struggling between the clouds, Frances folded her arms yet more closely in the woollen garment, and once more began that quick pacing up and down as though finding in it some alleviation to her mental distress.

The path was covered with a soft earth composed of decayed leaves, pine needles, and the sheddings of the yew-trees, so that her feet fell noiselessly. But the path in the shrubbery was gravelled, and before she had taken half a dozen turns on the space between the wicket and the yews, she heard some one on the other side of the laurels who was evidently coming toward her.

She paused waiting to see who it was.

And when Abel the old nurse, her muslin apron thrown over her shoulders as a protection against the cold, appeared, a faint expression of surprise came into her face.

"My dear," and the tiny little old woman came toward her, shading her eyes as though even the winter sunlight were too bright for them. "My dear, the mistress sent me to look for you. You must not stay out here, you who are not used to cold." Here a gust of wind caused the speaker to clutch a handful of laurel twigs for support, the print dress, muslin apron, and cap-strings fluttering in the breeze.

"Abel, you will take cold—you will get your death. Do go in," remonstrated Frances, hurriedly laying hold of one of the tiny arms, as if she would protect the old woman from the furious gust which just then rushed amongst the trees.

"Eh, my dear, it doesn't matter about me." And the sweet apple-blossom of a face was raised wistfully. "Old folk have to be carried off; it's only you young people that should stay."

Frances looked down at the old nurse, but did not speak, only smiled sadly at her.

Abel closed one of her withered hands over the young strong one that lay upon her arm, while she waited for the gust of wind to subside before speaking, then she said with earnestness and great emphasis—

"My dear, they made nothing out against my boy yesterday."

"Nothing, Abel." And as Frances answered, a cord seemed to be tightening itself round her heart.

"There's no one that can speak against my boy?"

"No one, Abel."

"I always used to say people didn't understand him."

"You and I know, Abel, that he meant well."

"My dear, that's just it, and you and I must always say those true words."

Here another gust of wind came, and the old woman clung to her companion's arm.

"You must go in, Abel, you must indeed. Mrs. Aschenburg would be angry if she knew you were standing here, without bonnet or shawl. See, I will take you as far as the terrace steps."

And so the two women slowly made their way against the wind, winding in and out of the shrubbery paths, up the terrace steps, across the broad gravel, each thinking of the secret which she possessed in the knowledge of that interview between Maggie and Sidney Aschenburg. Neither knew that the other possessed this secret, and neither felt that she could impart it.

There was a momentary lull in the wind, and the old nurse paused and looked up wistfully into her companion's face. It had been easier for her to determine whether she should be silent or not about that interview than for Frances. Right was always widely separated in her simple mind from wrong, and in this case—for, like Frances, she had come to certain conclusions respecting that interview and the crime of which Matthew Tindale was guilty— anything but silence could only have been wrong-doing in her eyes. And yet, now that the verdict had been given, she was not quite happy about the course she had pursued. With Frances, it seemed to her that by her silence she had compassed the death of a man. And so it was that she paused and looked up wistfully into her companion's face.

The continuity of retribution had touched her also, and caught her up in its folds.

There was a pause of a minute, and then silently did these two women who had loved Sidney Aschenburg pass into the house.

CHAPTER IV.

BONDAGE AND FREEDOM.

DAY succeeded day. The hail fell, the sun shone, the wind blew. Sometimes the sky was murky, and a grey veil stretched from horizon to horizon ; at others, it was partially covered with clouds that had jagged edges, and which every moment showed curious pictures that moved as dissolving views; now the profile of a giant warrior from head to heel ; now grotesquely shaped creatures that chased a deer whose antlers only rose from the billowy scudding mass. After this came hills and dales of a fair white land, then new forms and shapes that slowly grew and slowly changed again. But there were days on which the sky held itself bravely, and the clouds parting, a goodly flood of sunshine passed through, which, even if it had little warmth, was cheerful and bright. And the nights following these days were quiet and peaceful; sometimes there would be a little frost, and the stars would glimmer brightly, or the clouds that had given way to the sunshine would unroll themselves and spread their fleecy darkness over the heavens. Of course there were nights on which the wind blew fiercely, dashing the rain or sleet or hail against the windows, or down the chimneys, where by its faint hiss those who sat by the fireside were made aware that "it was a night outside." And there were other nights on which the wind only blew threateningly. But no matter how the stars were shrouded, or the rain fell, or the wind drove, the day, like some vast, irresistible piece of machinery, always followed the night, and then night came again, and then swift, as it seemed, was born another day.

So they passed until the last one came to Matthew Tindale.

The grey twilight of evening crept from its hiding place into the narrow lanes and alleys of the city. Outside in the country it was a little longer in showing itself, even near the hedges and trees, its favourite places of resort; but where men had huddled their piles of brick and mortar close together, it was born before its time.

It had come into the place where Matthew, seated on the edge of a low bed, one elbow on his knee, was shading his face with his hand, so that it could not be seen by the warder who sat on the other side of the cell, and who from time to time regarded his charge curiously, wondering whether he were asleep.

The convict's other hand lay half-open, its muscles relaxed; but there was no sound of regular breathing, no sudden droopings of the figure by which sleep is accompanied. For an hour and a half he had sat thus.

He had been feverish and restless during

the afternoon, pacing the cell for a few minutes and then throwing himself down on his bed, only, however, to rise from it almost immediately to renew his pacing. Or he would sit on the low stool provided for his use, stretching out his limbs in a distracted kind of way, now this leg, now the other. Then he complained of the closeness of the atmosphere, and loosened the prison dress which he wore. Finally he asked for the window to be opened, and it was then that he sat down upon the edge of the bed, and, covering his face with his hands, dropped into the attitude which, being kept so persistently, had caused the warder to wonder whether he were asleep or awake.

Faint sounds came floating through the window from the distant street; the tramp of footsteps, muffled until they seemed like the far-off murmur of running water, or like wind that rustles through leafless far-off trees. And to this, which was as a perpetual accompaniment, was added the roll of carriages, which died down, then rose again, growing louder or at times ceasing abruptly as some side street was turned into. Once a shrill laugh had risen above the faint, undistinguishable sounds, derisive and long-enduring; and the convict must have heard it—it was soon after he seated himself on the bed—for a faint tremor ran over him from head to foot, and the hand which was lying half open across his knee closed for an instant, the nails biting the palm as if he had been struck by a sudden twinge of pain.

The daylight faded slowly out of the cell, and the man who was seated on the bed became enveloped in shadow.

The sound of the muffled tramp of footsteps that came through the open window grew louder, with signs of hurry and idle excitement, and the voices of boys could be heard calling to one another, and now and then the shrill tones of a woman. Presently this increase of sound subsided, and the dull hum and the broken roll of carriages could be heard. In the far distance a faint booming rose with regular beats, with an occasional note from some high-sounding musical instrument. The sound of footsteps and the sound of voices grew louder, and the booming of the drum steadily increased until other notes beside those high ones could be heard, while above the muffled tramp of the feet in the street came the regular beat of the footfall of marching men.

Then the lower notes and the tune that was being played became distinguishable.

Here a voice in the street took up the words of the tune—

"D'ye ken John Peel with his coat sae grey?"

and another caught it up—

"D'ye ken John Peel at the break of the day?"

and then another and another—

"D'ye ken John Peel when he's far, far away,
With his hounds and his horn in the morning?"

The man sitting on the bed began to tremble from head to foot.

Nearer and nearer came the regiment of marching men until the music clashed loud, joyous, and triumphant. Snatches from many of the verses were now caught up, and flung about irrespective of each other. Now a fragment of the chorus, now a scrap concerning the hounds—" Ranter and Royal, and Bellman so true." Nearer and yet nearer came the regiment, louder and louder played the band, the music rising higher and yet higher, with the throb as of a passionate and mightily pulsating human heart.

The man sitting on the bed suddenly lifted his head, and the hand which had been shading and supporting it fell nervelessly beside the other. His chin was stretched out, and his eyes were full of fire.

The warder watched him attentively, for now that the position had been changed, the head of the convict had been lifted out of the shadow.

Suddenly Matthew Tindale sprang to his feet—and what a splendid man he looked

—his chest expanded to the full, his head towering, his great hands clenched as though they were of wrought iron. His lips were firmly closed, and he breathed heavily, his whole attention riveted on the sounds which now came rolling in from the street. Then he suddenly threw out one hand, and laid it heavily upon the wall, as though he would thrust the masonry aside.

" Now, then, no gammocks," called the warder, speaking with a strong southern accent, and moving in his seat as if debating whether he should rise or not. " You've been quiet hall along, so go on quietly to the hend."

But Matthew did not hear him. He was deaf to everything but that din of sound. Deaf and blind. He saw no restraining wall of prison cell. His native moorland had opened suddenly before him with the grand Pennine range of hills rising to the clouds. He felt its breezes blow upon his face, the strong exhilarating breezes of the hills. He felt his veins answer responsively, and tingle with the same strong life. He became suddenly maddened by the desire for freedom, and the mighty tide of pent-up emotion, which had been kept under for so long a time, flooded his soul. Oh, for the old life, for the old home! And Matthew raised his other hand—he had become conscious now of the narrowing walls, and in a fit of delirium, thrust himself against the masonry with all his strength. To be free again—to be on the moorland—to awaken! Yes, surely he had been dreaming a hideous nightmare—he would awaken himself, he would rouse himself.

"D'ye ken John Peel with his coat sae grey,
D'ye ken John Peel at the break of the day?"

Voice after voice took up the words, and the band clashed out its stirring harmony.

The breath was coming from Matthew's chest in thick hot gasps, and the sweat was running down his limbs as they shook and trembled with the violence of the force with which he leant against the wall. He felt as if

the music had driven him raving mad; as if
it had awakened in him such a desire for freedom and for life as was like to destroy his
brain. To be again in the old home! To
have once more the round of peaceful days
and nights! To be with his sister and his
parents—and ah! God, to be able to look once
more into the face of the woman he loved.

The hands with their up-heaved trembling
muscles were here lifted from the wall, and
Matthew reeled back a pace or two.

"Come, no 'igh jinks! I'm too hold a bird
for that." And the warder rose from his seat
as he spoke.

Matthew turned his face toward him, and
the gas being at that moment lighted in the cell,
all the signs of his mental agony were visible.

"To-morrow I shall be free," he said
hoarsely. "To-morrow you will be able to
keep me no longer. You are sending me out
into some place—you don't know where, an' I
don't know where—but any way I shall be
free."

" There's been no reprieve. Don't go and build your mind hupon that."

"Listen ! " And Matthew lifted his hand toward the open window. " That tune has made me tear and rive to get away. It has made me mad. I did not know till I heard it how much I wanted to live."

The music was getting each moment more indistinct, and the dull thud of the marching men was rising above it, like some heavy instrument beating time. The voices of the singers were far away, and only the high notes and the booming of the drum could be clearly heard.

" I hear nothing particular in the tune," returned the warder after he had listened for a few seconds with immovable face.

" Don't ye ! To me that tune is the grandest one on earth."

" Well, tastes differ, as the cat said to the fiddle."

Matthew stood with head uplifted and ear turned toward the window.

Fainter and fainter became the music, until at last only a note here and there could be distinguished, mingled with the distant booming of the drum. Gradually, moment by moment it melted, until at last nothing of it could be distinguished, and there remained only the soft murmur of voices and of footsteps from the street.

Still Matthew did not move. He was thinking again of the moorland; of its sunshine, of its cool breezes; of the singing of its thousand larks. And the expression upon his face became more placid, and he closed his eyes for a brief space. He was very tired; life had proved too much for him; he had meant, ah! how had he not meant to live it —and now? But to-morrow he would be free, and he would go to sleep. Yes, to sleep. For how long? He was very tired. Perhaps he would sleep for a thousand years!

And then without another word he turned, and sitting down once more on the edge of the bed, buried his face in his hands.

BOOK IX.

CHAPTER I.

AFTER FIVE YEARS.

It was early morning, and the smoke of the great city had not yet invaded the bit of common that lay between the cottages and the railway embankment. The sun was shining, the air was pure and clear, and the breeze which came blowing in from the country brought with it the fragrance of newly mown hay.

A woman was standing on the cinder-path that divided one of the cottage gardens into two portions, her back to the sun, her form held erect, while her head, with its masses of dark hair gathered into a knot upon her neck, was lifted slightly as she gazed far northward over the embankment. And the passers-by turned to look at the profile which was silhouetted sharply against the brick wall of the cottage, and at the head and shoulders which were thrown into relief by a broad mass of light; and some of them wondered because of her grace, her dignity, and her beauty.

A fair-haired child clung to her dress, vainly endeavouring to attract her attention; as, still gazing northward at the fleecy clouds that lay in a long low line across the sky, she put out a hand from time to time to smooth the curly head, or hold one of the little fat arms, until the child, with a child's restlessness, drew it away.

And what was it that the woman saw with that far-off rapt expression?

Minute after minute passed, and the eyes which usually were so full of sadness slowly brightened; their heavy dreariness little by little borne away, as twilight shadows are borne away by the dawn. And the low broad forehead became smooth and clear; and the lips, which too often drooped in weariness over a secret that must never be allowed to escape them, parted more than once in a smile, until at last the woman sighed, and the smile spread itself over the face like a gleam of sunshine.

Her life had been laid down, and must never be taken up again.

She was content. Her life—all that she had loved—had been given that others might live. Did she regret it? Did moments ever come to her in which, like a tired weary child, she yearned for her mother's arms to be folded round her? Did she ever sicken and long for one glance into that brother's face, for one smile to be given in answer to hers, for one greeting to come in his much-loved voice? Most like—most like.

Were there not times in which she turned her face into her pillow at night, and crushing her mouth into its folds that her cries might not disturb the child at her side, would writhe

and pray that she might have strength to hold
to her course; that the life once laid down
might never be taken up by her again. And
in the morning she would go out of the
little cottage, and standing with her face
turned upon the scene which memory painted
for her with loving hand, would strive to hush
the deep crying that had been awakened in
her heart, sometimes rocking herself to and
fro with her hands folded on her bosom,
while her breath came with deep hard-drawn
gasps. Until at last the vision which had
been conjured up for her laid itself as a balm
upon her sick soul, and the hands would slip
quietly from her bosom, and the rocking to
and fro would cease. Yes, she could bear it,
she could bear it all, she told herself. And
her heart would go out with tender yearning
to that far-distant home, and a quiet sober
happiness would fill it, as she forgot the cost
by which peace—the peace which, by her own
upholding, as she believed—had been brought
within its walls.

And so in the early morning she stood there looking northward.

Meanwhile the sunlight shone upon a woman who sat by her fireside, widowed and childless ; and the breeze swept over a border city, and round the towers of a gaol, and upon the grave of a convict, over which the towers of that gaol kept sentinel.

THE END.

PRINTED BY WILLIAM CLOWES AND SONS, LIMITED, LONDON AND BECCLES. *S. & H.*

www.ingramcontent.com/pod-product-compliance
Lightning Source LLC
Chambersburg PA
CBHW031953060726
47497CB00016B/1600